I0627597

A Spicy Predicament

Eugeena Patterson Mysteries, #6

Tyora Moody

Tymm Publishng LLC

A Spicy Predicament
A Eugeena Patterson Mystery, Book 6

Copyright © 2023 by Tyora Moody

A Spicy Predicament is a work of fiction. Names, characters, places and incidents either are products of the author's imagination or are used fictitiously. Any resemblance to actual persons, living or dead, events, or locales is entirely coincidental.

Published by Tymm Publishing LLC
www.tymmpublishing.com

Paperback ISBN: 978-1-961437-04-3
Ebook ISBN: 978-1-961437-06-7

Cover Design: TywebbinCreations.com
Editing: Felicia Murrell

Chapter 1

I think I've swayed my hips more in my old age than when I was younger.

Eugeena, you still got it, girl!

The man in front of me wasn't moving too bad either. Amos Jones had his two step game going strong like a man twenty years younger. Even with the lights shimmering off his bald head, I could picture how good looking he'd been back in the day. He was still handsome in my book. Aged like fine wine!

Both formerly widows, Amos and I, now Eugeena Patterson-Jones, had finally embarked on the honeymoon we should have taken over a year ago. Why so long? Well, certain events delayed our breakaway from our daily life. And there were the unexpected mysteries that I'd been determined to solve. But a sistah had grown tired of coming across people who committed unspeakable acts of evil, like murder. I'd experienced many melancholy days and a few nightmares that stole my sleep at night. The amateur sleuth hobby had not been how I planned to spend my retirement years.

Let's just say it was good to get away.

Tonight, the blues permeated the air, but I was quite giddy. An incredible feat, seeing as I was 550 miles away from my beloved home. I had spent all my life in Charleston, South Carolina, where I was born and raised. The most visited city in South Carolina, I'd seen people from all over the world in my hometown, but I hadn't traveled much outside the Palmetto State. I loved my Sugar Creek neighborhood where I'd spent more than half my life raising kids, being married to my first husband and in the past few years meeting my new hubby.

Amos proposed driving up to Music City, but I didn't see myself sitting in the car for eight hours. We were way too old for that. Conquering my trepidation for flying, we made it to Nashville, Tennessee, yesterday afternoon. I hated I missed church, but Amos caught a good deal on our flight out of Charleston International Airport.

Now, after a morning of sightseeing and an afternoon nap, we were, to Amos's amusement, hanging out in what I called a juke joint. The Blue Note Lounge, in fact, was very sophisticated with its textured walls, cushy seats, and mahogany tables. It was certainly no hole in the wall, not that I knew much about those kind of places.

The Blue Note's walls were lined with portraits of musicians, both famous and local. Although it was called the Blue Note, in addition to the blues, tonight we'd heard everything from Motown classics to jazz. While the lounge band wrapped up a lively number, Amos held his hand on the small of my back guiding us back to our table. I wasn't sure how we were lucky enough to be seated near the stage. In the corner to our right was an old jukebox. In between the band's sets, someone would push buttons keeping the atmosphere festive.

Now that we were seated, I had a chance to see the beautiful singer dressed in a dazzling royal blue dress. She'd delighted the crowd and was ending her set with "What a Difference A Day Makes," which I recognized as one of my mama's favorite songs. Mama loved Dinah Washington. It was one of the few things I remembered about her.

Our server swung by. Her big smile lit up a round face. She wore her hair in box braids that were swept up on top of her head.

"Y'all want your drinks refilled?"

While others were drinking spirits, I wasn't trying to be too adventurous. Besides, I wasn't an alcohol drinker, the taste never appealed to me. The Blue Note Lounge served food, and I had a tall, sweet tea with a basket of some of the best chicken fingers I'd had. Almost rivaled our favorite place back home, The Chicken Shack. Just enough spice to ignite my senses, but not too much to leave me up with heartburn later. The server poured more tea for me and brought Amos another craft beer.

"Ladies and gentlemen, can I have your attention?" I peered toward the stage. A young man had walked out on the stage, his smile dazzling in the spotlight revealing beautiful white teeth. I'd noticed the standard dress at the Blue Note Lounge seemed to be a black shirt, black jeans, and cowboy boots. There was an older announcer who introduced singing acts throughout the evening, but something about the younger announcer felt familiar to me.

He continued. "The person you've been waiting to see is ready to hit the stage. She's a favorite here at the Blue Note." Then he pointed to the crowd. "Are you ready?"

I bellowed out, "Yeah," like the others around me. I'd been looking forward to this ever since Amos showed me the two tickets he purchased. After so many years, I would finally get to see a childhood friend.

Cinnamon Waters.

Cinnamon stepped onto the stage as the crowd roared with excitement. Cinnamon and I were the same age, but she seemed much younger than me, defying her sixty-three years. She sported a honey blonde ponytail which was pinned back with a large red bow. She wore a short, sparkly red dress that hugged her curves in all the right places. I sure would like to know how she was able to keep that figure. She smiled and waved at the audience.

"How y'all doing out there?" As her name implied, Cinnamon's voice was sweet with a touch of spice. "So good to have you here. I have a few of my favorites I'd like to share. How does that sound?"

The audience responded in one accord.

The guitar player started a few chords followed by the rest of the band. As Cinnamon sang, her voice was just as I remembered when we were girls in the choir. Now it was more powerful, more soulful, and full of emotion. Moving with the rhythm of the music, Cinnamon slowly swayed her shoulders throwing her head back. Cinnamon's sultry voice mesmerized people of all ages and races.

By Cinnamon's second set, the crowd seemed to have grown around us. I hadn't paid much attention to all the tables filling in, but I assumed it was a pretty good crowd for a Monday evening.

I felt so proud of my friend. This woman was one of my closest friends at one time. Back then, she was shy and timid. But there was no sign of that young girl tonight.

Cinnamon asked, "Can you bring up the house lights? I want to see who's with us tonight." The overhead lights slowly flickered on across the lounge. She walked to the edge of the stage and patted her glistening face with a handkerchief. "Ah, yes, you all look beautiful."

Cinnamon placed her hand over her eyes to shade them as she scanned the room. To my surprise, our eyes met.

She pointed at me. "I see a special friend is here tonight."

I grinned and waved.

She sauntered over to the stage nearest to our table. "It's so good to have you here, Eugeena. This next song is for you, my dear friend."

I grabbed Amos's hand, tears filling my eyes. I whispered, "How did she know I was here?"

Amos winked like he had a secret.

To my surprise, Cinnamon sang "Amazing Grace." Her voice washed over me like warm water. As she sang, I closed my eyes, envisioning sweet memories from our childhood. This was a song Cinnamon's late mother used to sing. After she finished the song, she blew me a kiss. The crowd cheered and clapped, and I blew her a kiss back.

Cinnamon disappeared behind the curtains. The young man who had announced her showed up at our table. "Eugeena Patterson."

"Yes."

"Ms. Waters wanted me to give you a backstage tour."

"What?" I looked over at Amos. "Did you know about this?"

Amos grinned. "I've been busy over the past few weeks. You were worried about what I was doing. Told you I was making plans."

My hubby may have outdone himself. In all honesty, I was grateful to see Cinnamon onstage, but she was a world traveler, and it'd been some years since we last saw each other. In fact, the last time I saw her was six years ago at my late husband Ralph Patterson's funeral.

We rose from the table and followed the young man. Something about the young man seemed familiar, and I couldn't help but be nosy. "Are you related to Cinnamon?"

He turned and smiled. "She's my grandma."

I sucked in a breath as another memory hit me. "I knew it. You remind me of her older brother."

The man nodded. "Uncle Charlie. Yeah, I get that a lot. Too bad I never got to meet him."

"Yes, it's a shame. He was quite the musician."

"I heard. I play the piano like he did. Do a little singing too."

"Runs in the family." As we entered backstage, my thoughts went to Charlie Waters. He was my earliest crush. All the hours we spent playing out in the country, you get to know people, and there was no one as funny and rambunctious as Charlie. Charlie unfortunately passed many years ago before we all graduated from high school. "What's your name, son?"

"Jared."

"That's a nice name. You say you are a singer, too?"

Jared smiled. "I used to sing, but I mainly help manage my grandma's gigs."

Used to sing. He's so young.

"That's beautiful that you're helping out your grandma."

Going back behind the stage was a whole new experience for me. It was a tight squeeze. And a lot of people were standing around. I recognized some members of Cinnamon's band and her two backup singers. As we passed by, I noticed one of the backup singers and one of the band members, the guitar player, I think, were not too happy about something.

Could've been my suspicious nature, but the woman appeared scared and moved her hands around erratically. I caught the man grabbing her arms as if to steady her. I didn't have time to see anymore before Jared stopped in front of a door labeled "Dressing Room."

Jared knocked on the door, and then frowned. His hand stilled on the doorknob.

I listened closely. Someone was in there with Cinnamon.

The deepness of the voice indicated it was probably a man.

Their voices were raised, and though I couldn't tell what they were saying, it sounded like a full on argument to me.

I glanced at Jared and noticed his smile had disappeared. Deep lines marred the young man's forehead and his body seemed to grow stiff as a board.

An odd familiar feeling crept up my spine. Over the past few years, I'd developed a sense when something bad was going to happen. Amos told me it came from witnessing how people treated other people during their darkest moments.

I quickly prayed for peace and that I was wrong about a storm approaching.

Chapter 2

The shouting behind the door grew louder, Cinnamon's voice struck a different kind of tone than when she was onstage a few minutes earlier. Unconsciously, I reached for Amos's hand. I knew he must have sensed my nervousness because he squeezed my hand. It was hard to hear the argument clearly, but suddenly Cinnamon's voice shouted.

"Get out, get out of here right now."

I blew out a breath that I hadn't realized I'd been holding. "Is everything okay? Should we check on Cinnamon?" It sounded like it was a bad time for us to visit, but my friend might need our help. Arguments could escalate quickly into something else.

Jared held up his arm. "Can you stay here a minute? I will tell her you're here."

I glanced over at Amos, the same concern I felt was in his eyes. I responded, "Sure thing, son."

When Jared opened the door, I saw a man in black standing in front of Cinnamon. The man seemed to loom over her, his eyes laser-focused as Cinnamon pointed her finger in his face. Based on the height of my sons, I estimated the man to be at least six feet. He clutched a black cowboy hat in one hand and stood frozen in place taking Cinnamon's torrent of words.

"Just stop it! You betrayed me after all these years. There is nothing you can do to change what you did."

Before I could hear more, Jared shut the dressing room door.

I turned to Amos. "I wonder what that was about."

Amos shook his head. "Music artists tend to be a sensitive bunch. You never know, could be a disagreement over the performance, money, loads of things."

The temptation to put my ear to the door gnawed at me, but there were too many people backstage. Glancing behind me, I saw other people had grown quiet and lingered about, probably also hoping to hear more of what was happening behind Cinnamon's dressing room door. I was glad I wasn't the only one with a nosy nature.

Suddenly, the door was snatched open. Amos pulled me back as the man in black barreled out of the dressing room. He'd placed his cowboy hat on his head, making him appear rough and rugged, ready to get into a showdown. Towering over both of us, I realized he was even taller than I'd estimated. He was at least six foot four, and from the silverish scruff on his face and the crinkle around his eyes, he wasn't a young man. Might have been in his fifties or sixties.

He moved around us like he didn't see or care that we were standing there. We watched as the man sauntered through the crowded backstage, people parting like the Red Sea as he made his way to a door with an exit sign. The man pushed the door with such force that it banged open. It appeared to be a parking lot on the other side.

I hadn't realized I'd placed my hand on my chest until I felt my heart beating fast. When the exit door slammed shut, it felt like the entire backstage sighed in relief. All the people standing around returned to their own conversations or whatever tasks they were doing prior to the man's dramatic exit.

Cinnamon's dressing room door stood ajar, and I peered in to see Jared's hands on his grandmother's shoulder as if to comfort her. Cinnamon had sat down and was blotting her face with a tissue.

Our backstage visit felt so intrusive now. I started to tell Amos that we should just go, but Jared turned and smiled at us. Then he whispered in Cinnamon's ear, and she turned to face Amos and me at her door. Her face morphed from sad to elated as a smile formed, but her red-rimmed eyes could not hide the emotional turmoil from the past few minutes.

She stood from her chair. "Eugeena, it's been too long. Come in, both of you."

Cinnamon's dressing room was exactly how I'd seen them on television. There were bright bulbs above a wide mirror. She walked over and pulled me in for a hug. "I'm so glad you could make it tonight. It's about time you came to my neck of the woods."

"It's so good to see you, Cinnamon," I said, feeling a lump form in my throat. I wasn't one of those people who could just play things off like I didn't see or witness something. "I understand if this isn't a good time for you. We're in Nashville all week and can catch up another time."

Cinnamon waved like she was swatting a fly. "I'm sorry you had to hear that mess. That was Barry Jenkins, my former manager. Don't worry about him. He just wants to keep making a fuss because I got rid of him. Probably should have done it years ago."

Former manager.

I had so many questions, but it was none of my business.

Cinnamon directed her attention to Amos, giving him the once over with her eyes. "Introduce me to your new hubby. I understand he's the one who made you a world traveler all of a sudden."

I hooked my arm in Amos's. "You could say that. Meet Amos Jones, my hubby and partner in crime."

Cinnamon smiled. "I can imagine. Eugeena and I used to get into a lot of things when we were little. She was always a curious one."

Amos grinned. "I'm not surprised."

I elbowed him softly, grinning from ear to ear. I loved to learn. Being a social studies schoolteacher for thirty years, history was a subject I enjoyed, and that same passion transferred over to wanting to know details, in particular, little-known facts that people kept hidden.

Cinnamon asked. "You have to tell me how you two met."

"Well..." I smiled at Amos. "He wasn't hard to find, seeing as he lived next door. Both of us were widows and grew to like each other's company."

Cinnamon threw her head back and laughed. "Oh, my goodness! I love a good romance and love story. You know, the last time I was the one to get you out of Sugar Creek."

I grinned. "That's right! My first trip on an airplane. Cedric had just started his residency at the hospital, and Leesa spent the weekend with my aunts. Junior had just started practicing law at a new firm. Girl, that was an ordeal. All my children couldn't believe I was going out of town without them."

"You had a good time though."

"Yeah, once I got past the airport and the actually riding thousands of feet above ground trauma." I glanced over at Amos. "I did a little better this time. Window seats are not for me."

Amos quirked an eyebrow. "I wasn't around for the first flight, but I practically had to drag you on the plane after you were so determined we didn't need to drive here."

Cinnamon laughed, "Oh my. You two are a hoot! I would love for you to come to the house for a meal."

"That would be awesome. I know you inherited some cooking skills from Mattie." Cinnamon's mother had been quite a baker. It surprised no one she'd named her only girl after a spice. If Mattie Waters had her way, Charlie would have been named Chocolate, but her husband made sure he had a respectable name, Charles, Jr.

"Amos has quite the agenda for us."

Grinning, Amos spoke up, "Yes, next week we will visit Memphis and see the National Civil Rights Museum."

Cinnamon clapped her hands together. "Oh, that means I may get to see you again. I'm performing on Beale Street next week, too."

"Will we?" I looked at Amos. He tried to show me all the stops he'd planned, but I told him I trusted him and just surprise me along the way. Amos had already knocked it out of the park for me tonight. Anything else would be a bonus.

Amos nodded. "When Eugeena mentioned to me awhile back that she knew you growing up in South Carolina, I looked up your tour dates. I think we can make time to see you next week too. We're checking out here in Nashville on Sunday morning and driving to Memphis to spend the rest of our days in Tennessee."

All the previous tension from before completely left my body as my amazement at how wonderful this man truly was hit me again. "You have truly outdone yourself."

A sharp short sound had us all spinning toward Cinnamon's shut dressing room door. Then another sound made my heart pound in my chest. With wide eyes, I whipped around toward Amos, his face drawn as he uttered, "Those were gunshots!"

Cinnamon moved toward the door with a gasp and a frantic cry. "Where's Jared?"

A wave of dread and terror crashed through me, paralyzing me with fear.

Not here. Not now. Not during our honeymoon!

Chapter 3

Lord, this could not be happening.

I glanced at Amos who gripped my hand. I hoped we were mistaken about hearing gunshots, but I'd heard that sound before. A few years ago, my neighbor's beloved son had been shot. Amos and I both heard it, even saw the car that sped away from the crime scene.

Cinnamon moved toward the door faster than I'd imagined she could move. "I need to go. Jared needs me."

I hadn't even realized Jared had slipped quietly out of the dressing room while we talked.

Amos quickly stepped into her path and held up his hands. "We have to stay here. We don't know if there's an active shooter out there." He might have been retired but the policeman in him appeared when the situation called for it.

Cinnamon tried to sidestep Amos, but he blocked her.

She swore. "His mother would kill me if anything happened to him."

I touched Cinnamon on her arm. "We should listen to Amos. He's a former cop. He knows what do in these situations." I peered at him. "You really think there's an active shooter?"

Amos raised his shoulders. "You know this can happen anywhere, especially where there is a population of people. Anyone who's having a bad day or just decides to take others out." He pulled out his phone. "Someone may have already called 9-1-1, but I want to be sure to give them a call too."

Cinnamon held her head in her hands. "Why, Lord? All these people from all over the country. Who would just come and shoot up this place?"

Amos moved us back away from the door, and then checked to make sure the lock was engaged. "Let's just hang tight to see if the shooting stops."

We huddled in the corner away from the door for what felt like a long time, but it could have only been sixty seconds. Our breathing was the only sound in the dressing room other than the hum of the light bulbs above the vanity mirror.

No more shots rang out.

Cinnamon twisted her hands, her lips moving, "Please, Lord, let Jared be okay."

"He'll be okay." I couldn't be sure, but Cinnamon's fear was contagious. "It's wonderful your grandson is working with you."

Cinnamon peered at me. Her honey blond hair, which I assumed was a wig, hung over her eyes. "Yes, it's been good to have him around. His mother didn't want him to do this."

"To help his grandmother?"

Her laugh was harsh and bitter. "She didn't want him to be in the music business. He's such a brilliant boy and I knew what he needed. He needed to be around music again. Boy been singing since he was a small thing."

I nodded, "Jared mentioned he was your manager now. I know I shouldn't pry, but that man, Barry Jenkins, he didn't appear too happy."

Cinnamon closed her eyes and seemed to tremble slightly. "He'd been my manager for over twenty years."

"That's a long time. What happened?"

"Money. He's still claiming he didn't steal from me, but he was responsible for managing royalties from albums and making sure I got paid for gigs like this one tonight. I don't know what he got himself into, but he didn't have to steal from me. All he had to do was ask. I can't stand people sneaking around me."

Amos asked, "Did you have some proof?"

A wry smile crossed Cinnamon's face. "You really are a cop. No, but he can't explain what happened to all my hard earned money. So I got rid of him. Jared stepped up."

I frowned. "He has to be in his early twenties. Seems like his mother would be happy he has a fulfilling career opportunity working with the great Cinnamon Waters."

Cinnamon held her head like she was in pain. "He just turned twenty-two. He lost a dear friend. Broke him to pieces. Everyone can't handle grief. He's an only child like his mother. "

I nodded. "That's right. Lotus. I forgot she was your only child. I haven't seen her since she was a little girl. She wasn't with you the last time you visited Charleston."

Cinnamon let out a deep sigh. "Lotus and I stopped getting along about the time she turned twelve or thirteen. She left home right around eighteen. Got pregnant with Jared. I had to beg to see him. First time I saw him, he was already two years old. He's been dear to me ever since." She stepped forward toward the door. "Is it clear out there yet? I got to see what's going on. It's not only Jared, all my band members are out there too. They are all family."

Amos approached the door with his head cocked to listen for any sounds. "There hasn't been any more shots. I'm sure the cops have been called to the scene, but they still may have first responders come in first. Those guys are well trained, so let's move slowly and carefully."

I gulped thinking how quickly this beautiful night turned into something dangerous. Amos unlocked the dressing room door and slowly opened it. Noise seeped inside, a mixture of raised voices. Some were distraught. I could also hear law enforcement barking orders to maintain control.

Amos peered behind me, his face concerned.

Then a wail ripped through the open door. It was so loud, I thought it was Cinnamon. But she stood frozen in place by the sound. It was from someone outside. Amos pulled the door open wider and before he could stop her, Cinnamon shot out the door toward the commotion. I followed behind her with Amos close on my heels.

The side door stood wide open showing the parking lot. I could see people, many of Cinnamon's band members hanging inside and outside the door.

"What's going on?" Ahead of us, Cinnamon pushed her way through the bodies moving toward the door.

Trying to keep up with her, I pushed behind her, catching people sobbing and glimpsing tears as we passed through the throng of people. When we stepped outside, I saw we were on the back of the Blue Note Lounge. Flashing blue lights lit up the entire area, bouncing off the cars.

Ahead of me, Cinnamon embraced someone, hugging him tightly. I soon realized it was Jared. I grabbed Amos's hand as we walked over to check on the young man. He appeared much younger than he did earlier. His eyes were glazed as if he were holding back unshed tears.

I looked around, and then saw what may have shocked him. There was clearly a body on the ground. A police officer was pulling yellow tape around the area.

I strained my eyes and recognized the body was clothed in black, the apparent uniform for the night. But then I noticed a black cowboy hat on the ground. Was that ...? I turned my head toward Cinnamon as she held her grandson's face. He seemed to be mumbling something, but Cinnamon consoled him. "It's okay, Jared. It's okay."

With more insistence, Jared mumbled again. "Barry's been shot. He just fell. All that blood."

It was Barry! Cinnamon's old manager. Who would shoot him?

I looked at Amos, noticing his distraught face. He'd heard what I heard too. I felt bad for my hubby. I knew this wasn't what he planned for our first night out on the town.

He also knew me.

There was no way I was going to let this one go.

For the first time, I realized how much I didn't know about my childhood friend's life.

Where did Jared go when he left the dressing room?

Chapter 4

Barry was transported to Nashville General Hospital. Despite her anger at the man for supposedly stealing her money, Cinnamon insisted on being by his side.

Amos wanted us to go back to the hotel and I probably should have listened. But Cinnamon asked us to join her. Unsure how to say no, Amos drove us all over to the hospital in our rental car. Cinnamon sniffled in the back seat, while Jared sat frozen. I wondered how much the young man saw and if he needed some medical attention from shock.

Once inside, Barry was wheeled off to surgery and Amos went to find coffee while we sat in the waiting room. During the car ride, Cinnamon had removed her honey blonde wig. I was surprised to see her closely cropped silver hair.

She chuckled at my raised eyebrows. "My hair started turning gray in my thirties. Now it's completely sliver. I look like a grandma now."

I patted my salt and pepper hair, which I had twisted a few days before we left for the trip. The last thing I wanted to deal with was my hair on vacation. "We're not spring chickens. I'm so glad you've gotten to live your dreams."

After her brother's death, Cinnamon's parents moved her to Fayetteville, North Carolina. Really, they shipped her off to live with her grandmother. Cinnamon wrote to me about her parents eventually splitting up and getting a divorce. We were pen pals for a long time. I remember when she settled in Tennessee to start her music career. I'd settled into married life with Ralph and our first child, Junior.

I'd been deep in thought about the past. I wondered if Cinnamon was doing the same because tears spilled down her face again. She tried to wipe them away with her hands. I pulled a pack of tissues out of my bag and handed her some. "You really were close to Barry."

Cinnamon accepted the tissues and grimaced. "How can you tell?"

"Well, from what I saw of him, he was a good-looking guy, and he looked like your type. Tall, dark and handsome."

Cinnamon let out something that could have been a chuckle, but then turned to a moan. "He was more than a manager for a long time. Most people thought we would get married, but it just never worked out that way. I hated when I noticed money missing. I knew I had the funds, but the balance in my bank account wasn't matching. I kicked myself for trusting him. And being in love with him too."

"We can't help who we fall in love with, Cinnamon."

"Oh, Eugeena. I'm sorry. I don't want to burden you with my troubles. But it's been a little strange the past few months."

I perked up. "How so?"

She started to speak, but then looked around.

Jared sat in the corner of the waiting room still looking lost. He clutched an empty water bottle. Beside him sat the background singer I saw earlier. She rubbed Jared's shoulder. I looked around. Most of the band members who were onstage with Cinnamon were now scattered throughout the waiting room.

"How are your kids, Eugeena?"

Surprised by her abrupt change in the subject, I wondered what Cinnamon wanted to say to me and why she decided not to say it. I launched into an update about my family. "Junior's family has grown. The twin boys are almost teens and their baby girl is walking. Cedric got married. Him and his new wife, Carmen, are trying to have a baby. Leesa and I are getting along much better. She has two kids now."

"Sounds like you are a proud grandma." Cinnamon smiled slightly.

I grinned. "Yes, three grandsons and two granddaughters. It's a joy."

Cinnamon asked, "What about Amos? Does he have kids?"

"Yes, he had two daughters with his first wife. One of his daughters has a son. His oldest daughter, the one with the son, lives out in Seattle. But she lets him stay with us during the summer. We should see him in a few weeks. And Amos's youngest daughter lives next door in the family home."

Cinnamon nodded, and I grew quiet. I felt like I had just babbled on and on to fill the silence. I studied her band members. Everyone here wanted to know how Barry was doing. "You mentioned your band is family. Do you have other relatives in the business with you besides Jared? I noticed the woman with him was one of your backup singers."

Cinnamon glanced over and nodded. "Denise Hemingway, we call her Niecy. She looks like she's a part of the family, but I took her in after her mother passed away. Her mother used to be a backup singer for me as well. Niecy is a year older than Jared, so they grew up together."

"Oh, that's good that you could take her in after she lost her mother. How old was she?"

Cinnamon thought for a few moments. "Niecy? I think she was twelve. The car accident happened about ten years ago. Niecy's mama and I were close. Her death was hard. For a while, I had trouble singing. My band had become my family, and it's hard to lose a member. Niecy and I helped each other through the grief."

I realized Niecy was the young woman I saw arguing with the young man backstage earlier. I had assumed they were a couple, but now I noticed the young man stealing glances at Niecy. But she kept her gaze firmly fixed on Jared.

Jared's body language was worrisome. "Do you think Jared should get checked out?"

Cinnamon glanced at her grandson. "He'll be fine. It's just a blow to him, to all of us. Barry and I had our differences, but he's been in my life so long that Jared and Niecy think of him as an uncle."

"That makes sense." I commented. "I like how you surround yourself with a mixture of young and old in your band. Was that on purpose?"

Cinnamon shook her head. "Not really. Some members moved on. But Nashville is full of young people looking for opportunity. So sometimes you work with who comes in the door."

The young man who'd been eyeing Niecy turned on his heels suddenly and left the waiting room.

He'd caught Cinnamon's eyes.

With surprise, I watched my friend's face harden in anger. She muttered something under her breath.

I leaned in. "I take it that young man that left isn't your favorite."

"Tommy. Tommy Howard. He's my new guitar player. I only tolerate him because he's Niecy's boyfriend. She could do better than him."

"Looks like he's not happy she's not paying attention to him."

Cinnamon looked over at Niecy and her grandson. "Niecy is good for Jared. I know this is killing him. Barry always seemed like such a good soul. I don't know what happened to him."

"Did he fall on bad times? Financially, I mean."

"No, which makes it so troubling. Barry didn't just manage me. He has other artists, but I've been with him for the longest. He started his management career with me."

"Did Jared say he saw what happened to Barry?"

Worry etched across Cinnamon's forehead. "I think he did, but now he's not saying anything. Jared's seen a lot in his young life. I hate this happened to him. I hope the police don't bother him."

I cringed. "I saw one deputy take his statement, but a violent crime detective will probably want to speak with him too."

Cinnamon shuddered as if a cold draft passed by her. "Oh, Eugeena. He doesn't need that hassle. Now I wished I'd listened to his mother and left him alone. It wouldn't have been so bad if Barry had just walked away. It wasn't like we could prove anything or press charges."

I wondered about that. If the man had stolen money from her, how was he even allowed to show up backstage to harass her? And what were they arguing about before Amos and I arrived at the dressing room door? From the tidbits I could hear, Barry was still trying to prove his innocence.

Jared left us in the dressing room. If I were the young man, I would have had a few words to say to the man arguing with my grandma. I started to ask if Jared and Barry had any arguments, but Amos showed up armed with coffee. I took a sip of mine relishing the warm, bitter liquid.

Amos leaned in and whispered in my ear. "I know you want to stay and support your friend, but it's late, and we had a long day today."

This man knew me too well. I also knew what Amos really wanted to tell me was to not get involved. We were, after all, on our honeymoon.

Cinnamon spoke up. "I appreciate you both bringing me here. Amos, I know you planned a special time away from Charleston for you and Eugeena. I'm sorry about all of this."

Amos shook his head. "Not your fault."

Cinnamon sighed, her once impeccable makeup creased down her face, mascara making her eyes appear like a raccoon. "This is all my fault." She spoke so softly, I could barely hear her.

I grabbed her hand. "You can't take the blame for this."

Before I could let go, a doctor appeared with a suddenness that made us all jump. He was tall with a thick mop of dark curly hair that looked like it hadn't seen a comb in days. His eyes were red-rimmed and it was clear that he had not slept for a while.

"Is the family for Barry Jenkins here?" His voice carried a weight that suggested he had not come with good news.

Cinnamon stood up, her back ramrod straight as if she expected a blow. "Yes, Doctor. How is he?"

The doctor stepped closer. "It's not good." Keeping his voice low, the doctor said, "We have put Mr. Jenkins on life support. We don't know how long he'll be able to sustain himself."

Cinnamon gasped and buried her face in her hands. I put my arm around her shoulders, trying to comfort her as a sense of dread washed over me. Things had taken a turn for the worse. But what could we do about it? As much as I wanted to help, I knew this was in God's hands.

I felt bad for my friend that she had to suffer this way. Despite the falling out, Cinnamon still cared for Barry. He'd been a part of her life for most of her singing career. That was practically forty years.

I peered over to see how the rest of the waiting room reacted to the doctor's news. There were blank expressions on most faces except Jared. The young man appeared as devastated as his grandmother.

There was something odd about the whole ordeal, and I would need a good night's sleep to think it through. Cinnamon's first thought when the gunshots went off was worrying about Jared. Did she think someone was after Jared or that he was going to do something? She seemed really against anymore police talking to Jared. But I had lots of questions, and I knew the police would too.

I glanced over at Amos, who had the familiar resigned look on his face.

He was right to be concerned; I really couldn't let this go.

Chapter 5

I slept well. I'm pretty sure it had to do with my lack of sleep the night before. On our first night away from home, I called each one of my children. I even reached out to my two aunts, Esther and Cora. Everyone was excited that we finally took this trip. We hoped to have an enjoyable few weeks away from home.

So much had changed in twenty-four hours.

For one, I should have been more interested in the agenda Amos had lined up for us today, which included the Country Music Hall of Fame and Museum. Amos was excited to see all the exhibits, but my mind was still on what happened last night. Instead, I was struggling with guilt. While Amos showered and ordered breakfast, I searched my phone for any information I could find about Barry Jenkins and the shooting at the Blue Note Lounge. I managed to find a few search results about the shooting.

A headline jumped out at me. "One Critically Injured in Shooting at Famous Blues Club." The article explained that the victim, Barry Jenkins, had been taken to the hospital with grave injuries and that the police were still investigating the incident. My mind raced as I tried to process what I was reading. Since it was so prevalent now, last night Amos thought we could have been dealing with a mass shooter. The news reports made it sound like Barry had been targeted. Though he was killed near his vehicle, nothing appeared stolen.

All those people last night, I hoped someone saw something. The faster they found the shooter, the sooner Amos and I could get back on track with our trip.

The ringing phone interrupted my parade of thoughts.

All those people last night, I hoped someone saw something. The faster they found the shooter, the sooner Amos and I could get back on with our trip.

The phone ring interrupted my parade of thoughts.

Grateful for the distraction, I clicked over to answer the caller. Warmed by my daughter's face and number on the tiny screen, I added extra enthusiasm to my voice, even though I felt subdued. "Hey, Leesa. Everything okay?"

My daughter and I had grown closer over the past few years and I wondered if she sensed when I was distracted and about to go down the amateur sleuth rabbit hole.

"Hey, Mama, the kids wanted to talk to you. Please don't tell them they can keep Porgy."

I laughed, not realizing how tense my body had become. My decent night's sleep might not have been restful as I thought. In the background, I could hear a dog barking. Porgy was a Corgi that I inherited when a dear friend of mine died. I'd never had a pet before, but that pup had taken over my home. The dog loved being around the kids. After much whining, Leesa volunteered, or rather her kids volunteered to babysit Porgy while we were gone.

Leesa picked up Porgy the day before we left Charleston. I could tell she regretted the decision as she hustled her kids into their car seats and tried securing the feisty dog into her minivan.

After speaking with my very excited grandkids, Leesa returned to the phone. "I take it you're all getting along?" I chuckled.

Leesa sighed, "Mama, it's like having another kid in the house, but Kisha and Tyric love him. I kept running him out of their beds last night, but it didn't do any good. I believe he slept in the bed with Kisha anyway."

"That's Porgy for you. He thinks he's human."

"So everything is good?"

Yep. I knew there had to be a reason my daughter was calling me. "We saw my old childhood friend last night. Cinnamon Waters, you remember her."

"Oh, yeah. Doesn't she sing the blues?"

"That's mainly what she sings, but she sings other types of music too. It was good to see her." I didn't want anyone back home to worry, so I purposely kept the other activities from the night quiet. Hopefully, Barry getting shot would remain local news here in Nashville. If I told Leesa, she would blab to the rest of the family.

I already had Amos uptight with me.

There was a knock at our door, and Amos went to answer. A few seconds later, he rolled in a cart with covered dishes.

"Looks like we have breakfast. I will talk to y'all later. Tell the kids to enjoy Porgy and for them all to behave."

"Alright," Leesa said, "you and Amos enjoy yourself. I will try not to call and bother you anymore."

I clicked off my phone and watched as Amos lifted the covered plates off the cart and placed them on the table in the corner of our room. The hotel room was really nice, more of a suite with a designated eating area and another area with a couch and chairs in front of a large screen television.

Amos stirred earlier than I did this morning. We didn't talk when we finally made it back to the hotel last night, mainly because we were both exhausted. This morning, I could tell he had something on his mind. He let me get myself ready, but I could feel his eyes on me while I searched my phone.

He eyed me now. "Breakfast is ready. How are you feeling? You know we are an hour behind from our time zone."

"Yes, that's right. I'm missing that hour." Still wrapped up in the fluffy hotel robe, I shuffled over to him and rubbed his back. "Thank you for ordering breakfast. It looks good."

He turned and wrapped his arms around me, kissing me on the forehead. "Let's eat. We have a busy day planned."

We ate the stack of pancakes, eggs, and bacon in silence. I still couldn't shake off the events from last night and wondered if Barry had made it through the night.

I also had this burning need to know what happened and why he was shot.

"Amos, do you mind if we check in with Cinnamon?"

He put down his fork, shoulders sagging in defeat. "Of course."

"I know you have plans and I want to do it all, but I'm curious about Barry."

"Yes, I know. It's why I love you. You love a good mystery, but we're on our honeymoon."

"I don't want us to get too far off our plans, but I want to find out more about Barry. I felt like Cinnamon was holding back, like there was more to tell. And she was so worried about Jared. It all just seemed weird."

"Eugeena, I know you want to help, but you and Cinnamon haven't been in touch in years. Do you really think it's a good idea to dig around in her business and her family? I don't know. I think we should stay out of this. It's not our problem."

Just then my phone rang. I peered down at the phone and my heart started pounding. Cinnamon and I had exchanged numbers last night. I turned the phone screen towards Amos.

He looked at me, his mouth tight.

I put the phone on speaker so Amos could hear. "Hello."

"Eugeena, it's Cinnamon. I thought you should know Barry died early this morning. I could use your help if you could spare some time."

My heart dropped as my eyes locked with Amos, who lifted the palm of his hand over his forehead as if to ward off an oncoming headache.

I couldn't help but wonder why Cinnamon reached out for help, especially now that the man had died. Amos's concern combined with my many questions swam in my head.

What did she think we could help her with that the police couldn't do?

Chapter 6

The sun sat high in the sky, casting hot rays across the windshield and making the air conditioner work overtime. May in Nashville wasn't as hot and humid as Charleston, South Carolina, but the temperatures were pretty toasty today. It was still late morning, so I hoped we could hear Cinnamon out and continue with Amos's agenda by lunch time.

Amos followed the directions on the GPS to the neighborhood where Cinnamon lived. I watched out the window as we passed houses and streets, noticing that the houses grew bigger. The neighborhood showcased well-manicured lawns and houses two to three stories tall. While it wasn't a gated community, I could immediately tell from the neighborhood watch signs that this was an elite area.

The front of the home the GPS's female voice guided us to was smaller than the other homes, but it had one of the most beautiful, well-maintained gardens I'd ever seen. Cinnamon had done well for herself. Based on how she described her loss of money because of Barry's negligence with her finances, I wondered if she could still afford to live at her home.

Amos cut the engine, and we sat for a few moments, studying the driveway. I figured Amos had to be contemplating why we were here. I had to admit I had been doing the same. I didn't even know why I was getting involved. Sure, Cinnamon was an old childhood friend, but we had grown apart years ago. She led a very different life than me.

Someone opened the front door, probably suspicious of a strange car in the driveway. Then I saw it was Cinnamon. She waved at us.

I turned to Amos. "I'm so sorry that I'm messing up your plans for us."

Amos smiled. "Stop. We're in this together. Besides, I want to know what's going on too."

I patted his arm. "The retired homicide detective has been awakened."

"An investigation with you as partner has always proven to be interesting, Eugeena. Let's go talk to Ms. Waters. Maybe we can still salvage the afternoon with a few activities."

I said a prayer of thanks because I really needed to hear Amos's support. This man had been putting this trip together for months, only to see his plans go out the window after being here one full day.

As we walked up the paved walkway in front of the home, Cinnamon stood patiently waiting for us. First thing I noticed as we drew closer, that despite being home, Cinnamon wore makeup. I mean like makeup she would wear onstage. Today, she wore an auburn wig. I knew she didn't dress up to see us, so I assumed my friend needed to make herself feel good today. With Barry's death, we might not be her only visitors today.

Cinnamon greeted us warmly, hugging me first, and then Amos. "Thank you for coming. I appreciate both of you. Please come in."

She led us inside, past a stark, white and gray foyer before we settled into her living room. A bright white piano stood out in the corner, and a large painting reminiscent of the Lowcountry of South Carolina hung on the wall above it. Like the foyer, Cinnamon's living room was also shades of white and gray. The warmest elements in the room were the round pine coffee table and end tables.

Honestly, I expected her house to be a bit more homey and not like an interior decorator took over. Even with a few family photos throughout the room on the end tables and on a fireplace mantle, the house didn't scream Cinnamon to me. It was missing her spice, no pun intended.

Cinnamon sat on the gray chair opposite the white couch and motioned for us to sit. While Amos and I both tried to find a comfortable spot on the couch, I noticed Cinnamon fiddled with her hands as if she didn't know what to do with them.

"Would you like anything to drink?" she asked.

We both declined since we had just eaten a late breakfast. For some reason, today felt awkward compared to when we met in her dressing room last night. Perhaps grief had subdued Cinnamon's mood, or maybe it was us not knowing why we were here.

I think it was probably a little bit of both.

Cinnamon also didn't have the most comfortable couch. I have been on couches that sag and take you down into the cushions. This wasn't that kind. I wouldn't label it as hard, but it was way too firm. Maybe it was brand new. I shifted again for my lower back. That position wasn't working for my hips, and my feet were dangling. I had never been a fan of sitting in a chair that didn't allow me to place my feet on the floor. So, I leaned forward.

Amos didn't appear to be faring any better than me, and I was glad I wasn't the only one.

Not sure where to start, I pointed to the painting above the piano. "That's so beautiful. It reminds me of the Lowcountry back home."

A genuine smile spread across Cinnamon's face. "My daughter painted that a few years ago. She can sing but opted to express her artistry on canvas. Her talent brings back fond memories of my brother. Do you remember how Charlie used to draw charcoal portraits of people?"

"Oh, yes! He did a bunch of those of the church mothers one summer. I still have the one he drew of my mama. Mama didn't take many pictures, so that portrait is really special. Isn't it wonderful to see how family talents are passed on to our children?"

"It truly is. You should visit Lotus's art gallery while you are here. Her art collection is there, along with the works of some other artists"

Amos eyed me with a smile. "I'm sure we can arrange that." He didn't have to say another word. I knew from the pointed look he gave me, Amos wanted to get to the point. So did I.

"Cinnamon," I ventured. "What's going on? You said you needed our help."

She took a deep breath. "When I found out last night that Amos was a former cop, I wondered if you could help me figure out what's happening to me." Cinnamon's voice trembled. "And why now?"

Amos leaned forward, his forehead wrinkled. "We're talking about the shooting last night, right? Do the police have any leads?"

Cinnamon shook her head. "I don't know. They're not saying anything to me. But I have a feeling that I could be next."

"What?" Fear shot through my body making my heart race.

I wasn't expecting her to ask for that kind of help.

Cinnamon hesitated for a moment before speaking. "I've been receiving threats. Jared thought they were coming from Barry. It made sense because it started happening after I noticed the money missing from my bank account."

I frowned. "So you started receiving threats after you fired Barry?"

She nodded.

Amos added. "You told the police, right?"

Cinnamon sighed. "With the first threats I did, but they didn't take me seriously. I've been an entertainer for so many years. There are people out there who just don't like me for various reasons and don't mind letting me know. Sometimes I find things on social media, but this time it was different.

Someone sent letters to my mailbox. Whoever is doing this knows where I live."

"Do you have the letters?" I asked.

Cinnamon stood up and left the room. It sounded like she walked upstairs. I grabbed Amos's hand and lowered my voice. "What can we do?"

Amos shrugged. "I have no idea. Let's see what she has, but this really should be a cop matter."

A few minutes later, her heels tapped down the steps, and she returned with a small stack of envelopes. "Here. At first, I paid little attention to the envelopes. I get all kinds of fan mail, but I don't have the energy to answer, so Jared does it for me. Anyway, he found one and showed it to me. Then we discovered I'd received quite a few. You will see they are pretty aggressive. They were threatening me."

Amos said. "We probably shouldn't touch them too much. The police might can trace some DNA or fingerprints off of them."

"I gave the police the first two letters."

Amos asked, "What did they do about them?"

Cinnamon shook her head. "They just asked me if I had anyone who I'd argued with or upset. I couldn't think of anyone.

Even though Jared suggested Barry and we had several blowups about the missing money, I couldn't believe that it was him."

I asked, frowning at the letters. "What do they say?"

Cinnamon took one letter out of the envelope and unfolded it. She turned it around so we could read.

I squinted my eyes, expecting tiny writing, but the text resembled a child's handwriting, large and bold.

YOU SHOULD BE ASHAMED OF YOURSELF. YOU DESERVE WHATEVER HAPPENS TO YOU.

Cinnamon placed the letter down on the table and, with shaky hands, picked up another letter.

HOW CAN YOU STAND YOURSELF? SOMEONE NEEDS TO GIVE YOU A TASTE OF YOUR OWN MEDICINE.

I held up my hand. "That's enough." The contents of my breakfast had started doing cartwheels in my stomach. "This person seems to think you did something."

Cinnamon dropped the letter back on the table like it burned her hand. "I don't know what. I try my best to be good to people. Treat them the way I want to be treated."

I nodded. "I'm no expert here, but I would say Barry is off the hook for this one. Last night when you were arguing, he didn't seem opposed to telling you what was on his mind."

Amos nodded. "I agree. This is a person hiding behind some real loathing for you. And if it was Barry, the threats should stop now."

Cinnamon twisted her hands. "That's just it. Last night when Barry came to my dressing room, I confronted him to see what he would say. I told him it was cowardly for him to threaten me with silly letters. He denied it and said he would confront me."

Amos and I exchanged looks. My hubby's earlier hesitancy seemed to be replaced with curiosity now. He was hooked just like I was, and I wasn't sure that was a good thing for either of us. We couldn't hear the entire argument from behind the dressing room, but it would be good to know what Barry said to her. Those were some of his last words.

I asked. "Did Barry say anything else to you?"

Cinnamon hesitated for a moment, then said. "He wanted to talk today. Come by the house. He still was trying to prove he was innocent and that he wouldn't dream of stealing my hard earned money. Barry had other acts and other businesses. He didn't need my money."

I frowned. "Did he find out what happened to the missing money?"

Cinnamon nodded. "He told me he'd hired a private investigator to look into the money trail."

Amos crossed his arms. "Did he share anything with you about this investigator? It would be really helpful to know who it is and what they found."

"No, he didn't. But before he left my dressing room, the last thing Barry told me was to watch my back. He said everyone around me wasn't what they seemed."

That had my head spinning. "That was the very last thing he said to you?"

Cinnamon peered at me funny. "Everything happened so fast. I was yelling at him to leave, but yes, that's what he said. I have thought of little else."

Amos inquired. "So Barry tried to warn you last night that you need to watch out for someone close. Have you noticed anything else strange happening, Cinnamon? Are there any tensions between you and your band members?"

Cinnamon bit her lip. "My band is like my family, but like any family, we have disagreements."

I proposed. "There may be someone who is hiding how they really feel about you."

"Eugeena, you may be right. Barry's death is making me wonder if I'd been wrong. This could all be my fault for blaming

54

him? Maybe he didn't steal my money. I just assumed because he was in charge of collecting payments for me and the band. And I have trusted him with so much of my life over the years."

Amos shook his head. "Don't do that to yourself. You couldn't have known what would happen last night. I'm not sure what Eugeena and I can do. We can have casual conversations with people and ask how they enjoy working with you."

I nodded. "That's right. Most folks saw us at the hospital with you. Being an old friend of yours, we can strike up conversations. People's true nature often shines through, no matter how hard they try to hide it. We can at least listen objectively to folks around you and find out what's going on."

Cinnamon's eyebrows furrowed as if she was thinking really hard. "I can't think of anyone who would send me these letters. I'm not even sure now why I thought it was Barry. My mind is a mess right now."

I thought back to last night when Jared opened the dressing room door. The look on his face when he recognized the raised voices behind the door. How he disappeared while Cinnamon and I became reacquainted. I hated to ask, but I needed to. "Hear me out on this question. Was there any animosity between Jared and Barry?"

Now Cinnamon glared at me. "What are you trying to say, Eugeena?"

I held up my hands. "You asked for our help. I'm just trying to put the pieces together. It's quite possible someone else may have been stealing from you, someone close, like Barry said. A man doesn't just get shot randomly in the parking lot, Cinnamon."

Amos agreed. "Someone wanted to shut him up. Maybe they knew he wanted to reveal the true thief to you."

Tears swirled in Cinnamon's eyes. "It wasn't Jared. I know the police will try to pin this on him. That's why I reached out to you. But y'all are looking at him for this too. He wouldn't hurt a fly."

I thought about the hardened look on Jared's face last night. That young man didn't appreciate Barry berating his grandmother.

I insisted, "But what if Jared was trying to protect you? Everyone backstage could practically hear y'all arguing through the door."

Cinnamon opened her mouth to protest, but then a loud thump had us all spinning around. Sunlight drifted into the hallway outside the living room. That's when I realized it must have been the front door banging open.

A woman's voice rang out shrill and on edge. "Mom, where are you?"

My body stiffened, and I edged closer to Amos as a woman marched into the living room, straight toward Cinnamon.

"Where is Jared? What have you done to my son?"

Chapter 7

I've only seen pictures of her from when she was a little girl, so this was my first view of the adult Lotus.

Lotus must have inherited her height from her dad, because she loomed over her mother by a good three to four inches. Where Cinnamon's skin was bright, Lotus's features were deep chocolate and smooth. Her long silky black hair swung around her face as she walked into mother's living room with a purpose. Even with her face contorted in a mixture of anger and worry, she was stunning in a lavender strapless sundress.

Cinnamon jumped up from her chair to face her daughter. "What are you talking about? I haven't spoken to Jared since last night at the hospital."

"Something is wrong. Jared won't answer his phone. He called me in a panic late last night. He was babbling something about Barry getting shot. I could barely understand him. He was crying so hard. Then this morning, I heard on the news Barry died."

Lotus's voice cracked as her angry countenance crumbled. "Barry was like a dad to me growing up. Jared looked up to him." She jabbed red-tipped fingers at her mother. "This stupid falling out of yours with Barry these past few months has been horrible for everyone. And now he's dead. Who would shoot him?"

Cinnamon stepped back as if Lotus's words had smacked her in the face. "I don't know. I know Barry was a part of our lives for a long time. Believe me, I didn't want to think he did what he did."

Lotus roared, "Then why did you accuse him of stealing? He's been there all these years even when you didn't treat him right. Everyone knew how much he loved you, but you were too good for him."

I spun my head back and forth like I was watching a soap opera drama play out before my eyes. I rubbed my hand around my neck, which had grown tight with the tension.

Lotus paced the living room floor, her hands on her hip. She had inherited her mother's curvy figure, but if I'd ran into her somewhere else, I wouldn't have pegged her for Cinnamon's daughter. There wasn't a trace of family resemblance. Apparently Lotus's paternal genes dominated. I'd never met the man that was Lotus's dad. I just heard through the grapevine that Cinnamon had a child.

Cinnamon never confirmed, but I'd always thought her family left Charleston because of her brother's death. Charlie had been fatally stabbed during a brawl after a Friday night game. I used to wonder if it was more that drove the family away because Cinnamon ended up living with her grandmother at fifteen. Overnight, my best friend and her brother, my secret crush, had disappeared from my life. Counting the math, she had to have been sixteen when she had Lotus.

Lotus crossed her arms, now realizing her mother had guests in her home. She eyed us suspiciously. "And who are they? Friends of yours?"

Cinnamon waved her hand toward me. "This is Eugeena Patterson. She's a childhood friend from South Carolina. This is Amos Jones, her husband. They were at the Blue Note Lounge for my gig last night and also stayed at the hospital with me."

Lotus's face softened slightly. "I'm sorry for my outburst. I'm just worried about my son." Her eyes fell on the coffee table where Cinnamon had laid out the letters.

"What is this?" She bent down to read the letter Cinnamon had opened. "So you are receiving threats?"

Cinnamon frowned. "How did you know?"

Her daughter looked taken aback by the comment. "Jared tells me everything. That's why I'm worried that he's not answering me back. Why didn't *you* tell me about these?"

Cinnamon shrugged helplessly. "I didn't want to worry you. I was trying to handle it."

Amos asked, "Do you have any idea who would want to hurt your mother? Maybe someone Cinnamon has been oblivious to."

"No, I don't." Lotus glared at her mother. "You didn't think about the fact that Jared could be in danger. You know I didn't want him working for you."

Cinnamon closed her eyes. "I was only trying to help. You know how much Jared loves music. It brought him back to life after..."

I raised an eyebrow as Cinnamon glanced my way. Sensing that Cinnamon didn't want to say anymore in front of me and Amos, I said. "We can go, Cinnamon. Amos planned a lot for us today and it sounds like you should probably reach out to the police."

"No." Both mother and daughter shouted in agreement.

Amos frowned. "Why wouldn't you let the police handle it?"

Cinnamon huffed. "Just a few minutes ago, you both were asking questions about Jared. He has a right to be scared. He saw Barry get shot. I'm sure he's trying to process everything, especially if he found out Barry died."

Lotus exclaimed. "I'm sure he knows. It's all over social media now."

I inquired, "Where would Jared normally go if he's upset?"

Lotus sank in the chair nearest to her like her legs had given out. "I have looked and called around to his friends."

Cinnamon suggested. "Have you reached out to Niecy? She came back here last night to keep me company."

Lotus sat up in the chair. "I doubt she would pick up the phone if she saw it was me. Why did *she* stay with you last night?"

Cinnamon dropped her shoulders as if defeated. "Barry was important to her, too. You've never given Niecy a chance. She lost her mother while she was young. I think she turned out well despite the loss."

Lotus jumped up from the chair and practically growled. "Some of us whose mothers are alive are motherless, too. That might explain why they didn't turn out as well. You could have called me. Glad that you found the daughter you wanted in Niecy."

I gasped audibly before I could stop my reaction. Next to me, Amos stiffened, his posture poised to launch off the couch.

Good, Lord, things were tense between these two women.

"That's not true. I called you. I can't help it if you ignored my calls, which you tend to do all the time." Cinnamon's eyes widened and her voice tremored. "When are you going to stop this nonsense? You are a grown woman."

Lotus glared at her mother for what felt like a long few seconds. She turned to look at us. I guess whatever she saw on our faces made her regret her bitter comments. She lowered her eyes and mumbled. "I need to go. Let me know if Jared calls you. Tell him to call me ASAP so I know he's alright."

She stormed out the way she entered, leaving a heavy silence behind her.

I glanced at Cinnamon, whose eyes appeared glassy. "Are you okay?"

Cinnamon looked at me like she didn't really see me at first, then her eyes cleared and a small smile appeared. "I'm sorry for that. I tried to make amends with Lotus. We still have a lot of work to do."

"It's fine. Maybe we should get out of your hair."

Cinnamon nodded. "I appreciate you coming over. I need to plan Barry's funeral."

I frowned. That seemed odd, for her to be responsible for the man's funeral. "Really? Why would you do that?"

Cinnamon let out a deep sigh. "Barry had little family. His mother died a few years ago, and he was an only child. And I feel like somehow I owe it to him." Her voice cracked and tears streamed down her face. "I said some awful things to him these past few months. And last night, seeing him in that hospital bed, I started to doubt my assumptions. What if I've been wrong? I really wanted him to pull through, but now ... I can't fix it. The least I can do is lay him to rest."

I stood and walked over, placing my hand on her shoulder. "Are you sure you don't want us to stay?"

She shook her head. "I will be fine. Maybe you can talk to Niecy. Her and Jared are so close, I'm sure she may know how to find him."

The woman Lotus despised.

"That's the young lady who was sitting with Jared last night, right?"

Cinnamon picked up her phone. "Yes. She left early this morning before I got out of bed. She's such a sweet girl, just like her mother." Cinnamon gasped. "I don't even know if she knows about Barry yet. I found out from a friend who's a nurse at the hospital. Niecy is pretty busy during the day at her nail salon."

I turned to Amos before responding. "Sure, we can stop by and talk to her."

A small smile displayed on Cinnamon's face. "I can confirm her salon gives the best pedicures in this town. My treat!"

"Well, that sounds like a plan to me." I patted Amos's hand.

Amos raised his eyebrows, but he didn't say anything negative. I knew he wouldn't in front of Cinnamon.

He waited until we were outside and back in the hot car. As the air condition blasted us with slowly cooling air, Amos took a deep breath. "That was a lot more than we bargained for."

I agreed. "Well, I'm sure you didn't have a pedicure on your list of plans, but after all that drama, we might as well get some spa treatment out of the day."

And maybe track down Jared. Was he traumatized after last night or was something else going on?

Chapter 8

Amos easily found the salon on the car's GPS, but instead of driving to the salon, he headed back to the hotel. It was close to the middle of the afternoon now and I appreciated swinging by the hotel, our home away from home, to freshen up. Amos claimed it was an easy walk to the salon from the hotel. I'd been worried that we spent way too long at Cinnamon's house, but I knew Amos had become just as intrigued as me.

As we set off on foot, I didn't realize there were so many places within walking distance of the hotel. I didn't mind the walking since this was my favorite form of exercise around Sugar Creek back home. A few years ago, I'd been diagnosed with Diabetes II and I had taken off quite a bit of weight just from walking almost 10,000 steps a day. I didn't walk nearly as much, but I still monitored my sugar and was thankful I hadn't been prescribed insulin.

In about ten minutes, a neon pink and white sign, Niecy's Nails, flashed at us across the street. When the light changed, we shuffled over to the other side, crowded on all sides by other tourists. The moment we stepped inside, the strong scent of acetone filled my nostrils, but I welcomed the coolness. Rows of colorful nail polish bottles lined the walls. Two women, one behind the counter and the other, probably a patron, were giggling about something.

Beside me, Amos grumbled. "Do I really need to be here?"

"Nothing wrong with men getting pedicures, too."

"I'm the only man in here." Amos huffed.

I could see what he meant. From the view into the salon behind the plexiglass that separated the reception area from the service area, several nail attendants were at work but it wasn't very crowded. The salon was quite spacious, not small and cramped but very stylish with mauve walls and black leather chairs.

I glimpsed Niecy, who stood to the side talking to patrons.

The walls were covered in an array of pictures similar to the Blue Note Lounge. Having a gallery of people, maybe some famous, seemed to be a popular decor.

The receptionist beckoned us to come closer to the counter. "Come on in," she called out. "Do you have an appointment?"

Amos stiffened beside me as if he hoped we would be turned away.

"No," I said, "but your sign says walk-ins are welcome. Plus, a friend of mine is treating us today."

The woman flashed me a smile. "That's an awesome friend to have. What can we do for you today?"

I slipped my arm into Amos's hand. "We're visiting from out of town on our honeymoon. We would like pedicures."

With an even deeper drawl, the woman exclaimed. "How adorable! I love it. Let's get you two lovebirds seated right away. Niecy is going to want to meet you."

Interesting, because we want to meet Niecy.

Before walking back, Amos hesitated, eyeing the direction we were going suspiciously.

I grabbed his hand and whispered. "It will be fine. Remember, we need to get some information about where Jared could be."

Reluctantly, he nodded and settled into the plush leather chair. We removed our shoes and in a few minutes, water bubbled up in the tanks. Amos grimaced as the attendant took his feet and placed them in the bubbly, warm water. I smiled as I noticed the tension leaving his face.

"This ain't half bad," he said.

"I knew you would come around." I peeked over to see Niecy had finished her conversation and now walked toward us. "Welcome! I hear we have some honeymooners gracing our presence."

"Thank you! An old childhood friend of mine recommended you. Cinnamon Waters."

Niecy's eyes opened wide. "Yes. Cinnamon called me. She told me to give you the works."

"I'm ready!" I narrowed my eyes at her. "Weren't you onstage last night at the Blue Note Lounge?"

Niecy smiled. "Yes, I'm one of the younger background singers. It's been a privilege working with such a legend. Well, I've actually known Cinnamon all my life, but she has a different side to her onstage. Very exciting!"

I commented. "It's a shame about Cinnamon's former manager, and now Jared is missing."

Niecy stepped back as if lightly pushed. She glanced around, and then lowered her voice. "Wait, Jared's missing?"

"Cinnamon nor Lotus have heard from him. Maybe you know how to reach him."

She nodded her head, her eyes unfocused. "Yeah, I might know where he is." Niecy closed her eyes, and then zoned on my face. "And what about Barry? Do you know how he's doing? I stopped over to see Cinnamon last night. She seemed so down. I tried encouraging her that Barry could pull through. Then they could put the past few months behind them."

I glanced at Amos, my immediate thought that I may stir up a hornet's nest. Niecy seemed like a really sweet child, and she sounded so optimistic. I gulped. "You haven't heard?"

Niecy stared at me, her pretty eyes filling with tears. She started shaking her head and in a low voice, almost a whisper, she stated flatly. "He's dead, isn't he?" Her pretty face crumpled as she looked away. "I can't believe it."

I felt so bad as I watched the young woman turn and head into her office. Amos grabbed my hand, seeing the distress that I was sure was on my face.

Sometimes I really knew how to put my foot in my mouth.

Despite the tingling I felt from the peppermint lotion the attendant applied to my feet, my thoughts swirled. Cinnamon had been receiving threats about the same time she fired her long-time manager. Someone had been stealing money from her. Her grandson went missing last night after the shooting. I'd just upset a young woman in the middle of her workday.

What a mess!

Despite any perceived betrayal, Cinnamon had sat stoically in the hospital last night and wouldn't go home until her band members practically forced her to leave. I could tell she had deep feelings for Barry. I mean, she was planning his funeral.

After we finished, we went up to the counter and waited for our turn. The receptionist had disappeared, and another client waited patiently to pay. Finally, the receptionist returned. "How would you like to pay?"

The young lady ahead of us held up her phone. "Can I tap with my Pay App?"

I cringed inside. My daughter liked to pay for things like that. Everything was on an app. She'd gotten me to sign up for Pay App a few years ago, but I hardly ever used it unless Leesa needed some help with something.

We were next in line, and the receptionist smiled at us. "Did you enjoy your pedicures?"

"Yes, we did." I spoke up for Amos because I knew he wasn't going to admit it.

The receptionist beamed, showing off a toothy bright smile. "Well, you are all taken care of. You don't owe anything."

So, Cinnamon had treated us. I really appreciated her taking the time to do it, especially with all that was going on with her.

"I still would like to leave a tip for the attendant. Can we do that here?"

The receptionist nodded. "Yes, I will make note of their tips."

Amos handed over several dollar bills in cash.

"Is Niecy still here?" I'd been watching her office and from what I could tell, she'd remained closed up in there.

The receptionist looked puzzled. "Yes, she's still in her office. She looked pretty upset earlier. I will let her know you are walking back." She picked up her phone and sent a text.

I smiled at the receptionist. "Thank you."

Amos said nothing when I asked to see Niecy.

We made a single line back behind the plexiglass, passing the other patrons. I knocked gently on the frosted glass door of Niecy's office. "It's Eugeena and Amos. May we come in?"

There was a long pause. Then Niecy's muffled voice responded, "Come in."

When I cracked the door open, Niecy sat behind an oak desk, posture rigid, arms folded across her chest. Her eyes were puffy, lashes wet with tears. She stared at us warily. Amos slipped in behind me and closed the door.

"Are you okay? I'm so sorry to have to tell you bad news like that."

"It's okay." She said, "I knew he was in bad shape last night. It just doesn't make sense why someone would shoot Barry."

I eased into one chair across from her desk, glancing at Amos to signal him to do the same. I said gently. "Cinnamon is beside herself. She's scared too."

Niecy's gaze flickered between us. She swallowed hard. When she spoke, her voice was hoarse with emotion. "What do you mean? Scared?"

I wasn't sure how much Cinnamon wanted other people to know about the threats. Amos and I were to find out how people around her felt. Who could be the one responsible for sending the letters? We could be just wasting our precious time on our trip. So I opted to explain. "When someone is taken away from you, especially in a violent manner, it can be traumatic. Wouldn't you agree?"

Niecy swallowed and nodded her head. She grabbed a tissue from the corner of her desk and wiped her eyes.

I waited, giving her space to compose herself. Many times people liked to give their thoughts about a person who'd just passed, share any memories.

At last she took a deep, shuddering breath and said in a whisper, "I remember Barry from before. Before my mama died and I went to live with Cinnamon." Niecy swallowed again.

"Mama and Barry, they were...together, for a while." She gave a bitter laugh. "Barry was like a father when I was younger. He bought me presents and told me I was gonna be a star just like Cinnamon one day. He's always been there in my life."

"I'm so sorry, Niecy," I said softly. "I know you lost your mother and now losing Barry too. I'm sure this is a difficult time for you."

She glanced up at me through her lashes and gave me a tremulous smile. "Cinnamon gave me a home and a purpose." Her smile faded. "I guess I just wished that she'd heard Barry out instead of firing him. It seemed so unfair for Cinnamon to accuse him of stealing. She said some pretty horrible things."

I cocked my head to the side. "Surely she didn't wish him dead."

Niecy's eyes widened, and she held up her hands. "No. No. Nothing like that. But I heard her say she didn't want to see him again. She pushed him away. Barry was a good man. He loved her."

Interestingly, Lotus said something similar. Barry had been in Cinnamon's life for a very long time. That made the disagreement and assumed betrayal between them even more tragic. Their conflict had affected those around them, in particular those who thought of Barry as a father figure.

Since Niecy had been keeping Jared company last night at the hospital, I wondered if he said anything to her. If they were so close, maybe there was a clue in what he said and what was going on inside his head that now had him missing in action.

Just as I was about to ask, Niecy's office door banged open, startling us all.

Chapter 9

The sudden interruption had Amos jerking upright, his hand twitching toward where his service gun used to hang. I hugged my bag close to my chest as my gaze fell upon the young man who'd burst into the office. Even with the durag on his head, I recognized him from last night. He was the man backstage in a heated argument with Niecy as we passed by them on the way to Cinnamon's dressing room.

Were they just having a lover's quarrel?

I sure hoped this young man wouldn't continue the argument now.

I glanced at Niecy in time to catch her fear dissolve into raw anger as her eyes narrowed. She jumped from her chair, her hands fisted at her side. "Tommy, what is wrong with you? Don't you know how to knock? This is my office and I'm running a business."

Tommy shifted on his feet, his hooded eyes darting to me and Amos. His jeans hung low on his waist and muscles bulged from a white tank top. "Sorry, I thought you were alone. We need to talk...now."

Niecy shook her head. "I don't have time to talk to you. I need to figure out where Jared went."

I couldn't help but comment. "Seems like everyone is looking for Jared."

Tommy turned his attention to me. "Who are you?"

"Friends of Cinnamon's," I answered quickly. "She and his mother are looking for him. When did you last see him?"

Tommy hesitated as though he wasn't sure why some old woman was asking him questions. "Last night. We were all at the hospital." He cocked his head. "Now I remember you. You two were sitting with Cinny. I was thinking I'd never seen you before last night."

Cinny!

That was the first time I'd heard that nickname in years. The only person I knew to get away with calling Cinnamon that was her now deceased brother.

"Cinnamon and I were childhood friends in South Carolina. We've seen each other on and off over the years. My husband, Amos and I are in Nashville on our honeymoon."

Tommy raised his eyebrows, and then a sly smile crossed his face. He had ruggedly good looking features. When he smiled, a gold tooth sparkled from the side. "Congratulations and welcome to Music City. Sorry y'all had to come through and get caught up in Cinny's mess."

"Tommy," Niecy's low tone sounded like a clear warning, "stop calling her that. You know she doesn't like *you* using her nickname."

That didn't surprise me. I wondered how Cinnamon would react if she heard Tommy referring to her as Cinny.

Tommy shrugged like he could care less. "What? Barry used to call her that all the time."

Barry? That's interesting.

"He was special. And Barry's dead." Niecy hissed. "Let's just mourn the man and leave the past alone."

"What?" Tommy swore under his breath. "Cinny can't hide her head in the sand no more. She's going to find out all this time she's been accusing him that she's been so wrong. Then she's going to lose everything." Tommy walked closer to the desk, pointing his fingers at Niecy. "You know I'm telling the truth. The whole band is sick and tired of her. None of us have even been paid since Barry got fired. Jared doesn't know what he's doing. He put on a good game to impress his grandmother, but she won't hear us out or doesn't care. She's about to not have a band, or at least not have me. I bet Jared ain't missing. He probably ran off with the money from last night."

I glanced at Amos, who eyed me. I assumed he wanted me to keep my mouth shut, but I had no plans to interrupt. This was more informative than I could have imagined.

Niecy sighed. "Cinnamon knows the band hasn't been paid. She's still trying to recover from the stolen money. I think she was hoping Barry would confess and give it back."

Tommy huffed, "Right. Ain't like she broke living in that mansion. She can still pay us what we're owed. None of us wanted to go onstage last night. If it wasn't for you, we would have walked out."

Niecy walked around her desk toward Tommy. "Look, Amos and Eugeena don't need to know all the dirty laundry."

"I disagree." I said. "Maybe I can ask Cinnamon about it."

Tommy grumbled. "Someone needs to get her to see reality. We're all tired of the diva act. I'm surprised Barry lasted as long as he did with her. Poor guy, he did at least try to not only look out for her but all of us. He kept the band together."

"Sounds like all of you thought the world of Barry. I can't understand why Cinnamon felt he'd turned on her and stole her money."

Tommy shrugged. "I don't know. I haven't been in the band long, but others say that Cinny has gotten paranoid the last year. Maybe she's getting too old to do this anymore."

"That's a pretty disrespectful thing to say, young man." My teacher voice came through.

Tommy at least had the nerve to look sheepish. "No offense."

I thought Cinnamon said she'd been receiving threats for a few months. I could see how those letters would make her paranoid and distrustful of people. But could it have been longer? "What do you mean by paranoid?"

Niecy and Tommy exchanged looks. Niecy cleared her throat. "I wouldn't say paranoid. She's been in the business for a long time. It's all she knows."

Tommy looked at me, "She wants to stay relevant. Most of her original band members aren't with her anymore. She replaced them with younger people like me and Niecy."

In other words, she wants to not be old.

"That's not how it is." Niecy protested.

Tommy smirked. "Well, just like Barry, she didn't have great reasons to get rid of them."

"People grow apart, Tommy. You wouldn't be in the band if a spot hadn't opened up for you."

He grunted. "Hasn't been worth my time. So, where do you think Jared went? Still sounds mighty suspicious to me. "

Niecy sighed as though she wished Tommy would disappear. "I might know some places where he'd go."

Tommy huffed. "Well, let's find him."

Niecy snapped and pointed her finger at him. "You need to stay away from him. You've caused enough trouble for him."

Tommy shouted. "Me! Jared ain't no goody two shoes. You and the women in his family need to recognize that."

Niecy shot back. "We know him way better than you. I'm sure Jared knows nothing about the missing money. He mainly just keeps up with what Cinnamon needs. He never could be a real manager like Barry."

A muscle jumped in Tommy's jaw. "Yeah, I know that. That's what I've been saying. Either I get paid or I need to bounce from the band. I have other gigs I could do with a lot less drama." As abruptly as he arrived, Tommy snatched the office door open and slammed it.

We all cringed.

I felt sorry for Niecy. Her nail salon customers and employees had to hear all of that. And why was there so much animosity from Tommy about Jared? I thought I'd sensed something last night in the hospital waiting room. Was it possible Tommy was jealous of Niecy's friendship with Jared? As much information as we'd gathered in the last few hours, there were still so many questions, too.

Since the two didn't seem to mind that Amos and I heard their bickering, I mentioned, "I noticed you two backstage last night when we were on our way to Cinnamon's dressing room. Tommy appeared upset. Was that about not getting paid?"

Niecy's eyes opened wide. "Oh, I didn't realize you saw that."

Amos said, "Surely Tommy has another job like you do. Musicians don't make a ton of money."

Niecy sighed. "No, we don't. Tommy is a mechanic, but he probably owes someone money."

Amos raised an eyebrow. "He likes to gamble."

"Oh, yeah. He's a great guitar player, but his love for gambling often gets the best of him. A month ago, he borrowed some money from me to pay off a debt to one of the local bookies. I gave him what I could, but it was clear that he needed more. He wanted me to ask Cinnamon, but I wasn't about to do that, even if she can be generous."

Interesting that Tommy thought Cinnamon was loaded. I could see how he thought that based on her house. I wouldn't call her home a mansion, but the home appeared on the high end. I wasn't trying to be in my friend's financial business, but all of this fuss seemed to start with missing money.

I asked, "What do you mean by generous?"

"Cinnamon takes care of her people. It's why people stay loyal to her for so long."

Recalling what Tommy said a few minutes earlier, I said. "So it sounds like Cinnamon went through an abrupt change about a year ago."

"I guess you can say she has changed. She certainly wouldn't do the things she did a few years ago."

Amos's forehead wrinkled in concentration. "What kind of things did she used to do?"

Niecy leaned back in her chair. "Why these questions?"

Amos explained. "We don't know Cinnamon's world the way you do. You can help us figure out what's going on."

Niecy nodded like it made sense to her, but she still eyed us. "Okay. Well, for starters, even though she can be ungrateful, Cinnamon helped Lotus get that fabulous art gallery up and running a few years ago. It was her way of making amends with her daughter. And I'd been saving money for years styling and doing makeup for a lot of singers, but still didn't have enough. I didn't ask her, but without Cinnamon's help, this salon would still be a dream."

Something occurred to me while Niecy talked. "You worked with other singers. Are there any that don't get along with Cinnamon?"

Niecy squirmed in her seat like a kid who'd been asked to snitch. She blew out a breath. "This isn't news. Everyone in this town knows about the fallout between Cinnamon and Olivia Harris. The crazy thing is, they were best friends for so long. All of them, including my mama."

I frowned trying to absorb what the young woman was saying. "Olivia was a backup singer too?"

Niecy nodded. "Backup singer for over twenty years. Cinnamon fired her about a year ago. Sadly, that's how I got my chance. She also fired her long-time guitarist, Nate Parker. So those are two people who probably hate her. Well, I wouldn't say they hate her. In this town, when you're good, you can get work. Olivia got the best deal. She married the owner of the Blue Note Lounge."

Amos and I exchanged glances. "Really?" My mind whirled a mile a minute. "So, would she have been at the Blue Note the night Barry got shot?"

"Oh, she was there. Cinnamon ran into her right before going onstage. She was the woman singing before Cinnamon."

I recalled the bright skinned singer singing the Dinah Washington song. She reminded me of an older version of Beyonce. Well, she looked more like Beyonce's mom. Her voice was higher than Cinnamon's, not as soulful, but she definitely entertained the crowd.

Niecy picked up a stack of paper on her desk, tapped them against the desk, and then placed them down again. "Look, I really need to get back out there to the salon. I've been hiding back here long enough and I have a few new girls. I want to make sure they are doing things the way I like. I run a good business here." She stood and smiled at us. "I take it you both enjoyed your pedicures?"

Amos and I both stood. I was glad to stand since my knees had grown a little stiff. I gushed, "We absolutely loved the pedicures. Appreciate the service, and my condolences about Barry. He sounds like the glue that held things together for a while."

"Yes, he... did." Niecy stuttered. "It's a shame Cinnamon started seeing people as enemies all of a sudden. Barry tried hard to convince her to not let Olivia and Nate go, but she did it anyway. It demoralized the rest of the band."

Amos said, "You all sounded good the other night. People make things work even when they don't get along."

I nodded in agreement with Amos. "We'll get out of your way. Thank you for talking to us."

It was late afternoon now, and the salon had filled up since Amos and I arrived. As we exited the salon out onto the sidewalk, even more tourists sauntered up and down the street.

I hooked my arm into Amos's. "I appreciate you being brave and letting someone touch those toes today."

Amos chuckled. "They do feel good." He peered down at his watch. "Are you ready for something good to eat?"

"Absolutely. We missed lunch, and I'm famished."

"Well, now we can actually get back on track. There's a restaurant I wanted us to try not too far from here."

I smiled, glad to see some joy return to Amos. "Lead the way. My stomach is ready."

As we blended into the crowd, I still couldn't totally put my friend's troubles out of my mind. I realized since being in Nashville, how much I didn't know my childhood friend at all. I also wondered what started it all a year ago for her.

Something started happening long before the threats began.

Chapter 10

Amos and I settled into a table at the back of Ruth's Chris Steak House. After a long day, it was good that Amos had scored a reservation earlier. The man had planned everything. With all that happened since we'd been in Nashville, I felt bad that we'd drifted away from the reason for our visit.

The dim lighting and soft music created a perfect atmosphere for a romantic setting. The clink of silverware against ceramic plates brought a sense of normalcy that had been missing most of the day. After perusing the menu, I finally settled on the Sizzling Crab Cakes, while Amos ordered a steak filet. Once the server left us to get our drinks, I glanced over at Amos. He'd been quiet since we left Niecy's salon. I knew the threats against Cinnamon, her former manager's murder *and* her grandson Jared's sudden disappearance had consumed our trip.

I felt guilty about it, but I knew there must have been some reason this all blew up when Amos and I were in Nashville. It brought to mind a verse from Proverbs 19 I used to lean on during my time as a schoolteacher, especially those days when I wasn't sure I wanted to stay in the profession.

Many are the plans in a person's heart, but it is the Lord's purpose that prevails.

"So, I shouldn't have a problem getting you to come with me to get a pedicure back home." I teased.

Amos chuckled. "I've been known to step outside my comfort zone for you, but that might be a once in a lifetime experience."

"Is that so?" I asked, raising an eyebrow.

"Okay, it wasn't that bad, just don't go telling my buddies about our adventure."

I laughed. Amos hung out with other retirees like himself who worked in law enforcement for years. They were still a tough bunch often investigating cases. I'd been inducted as an honorary member.

The server placed our iced sweet teas and a steaming breadbasket in front of us. I reached for one of the buttery rolls and bit into it. We hadn't eaten since breakfast at the hotel, and I didn't realize how hungry I was until I savored the buttery bread, which practically melted in my mouth.

After a few moments, Amos asked. "What do you think we accomplished today?"

"We learned some new things." I twisted the napkin in my lap. "There's something that both Tommy and Niecy mentioned that's still bugging me. Cinnamon became paranoid almost a year ago. But the letters filled with those vile threats started coming a few months ago. And it's someone who knows her home address, which is really scary."

Amos took a sip of his sweet tea. "Yeah, I hope she still goes to the police again. There's no reason they shouldn't take her seriously. The timeline isn't adding up. Unless her paranoia is for another reason."

"What else could make her paranoid other than threats?"

Amos looked at me. "Suppose Cinnamon wasn't totally being honest with you? I know you both have known each other since childhood, but there's a lot of years in between and sometimes people are not who we think they are."

I frowned, trying to grasp what Amos was saying. "You think Cinnamon was holding back some information?"

Amos shrugged. "Someone thinks Cinnamon did something. It could have been a few months ago or years ago. We can't ignore the possibility that there's more going on here. Plus, there's a man who's been murdered and there's a good chance it could be related to whoever isn't happy with Cinnamon."

Before I could comment, the server brought our food. The plates were steaming hot, but we dived in. One would've thought we hadn't eaten in days. I needed the time to think. Amos brought up a good point, one that hadn't gone past me. I didn't really know Cinnamon anymore. I remembered the little girl from the country, the one I ran up and down dirt roads with. The preteen I'd sat next to in the youth choir amazed at how well she could harmonize and belt out a song, when I could barely carry a tune. The few times we'd met over the past forty years, I'd been more of a fan than a friend.

I sat back after cleaning my plate and wondered aloud. "I have to say the first time I visited Cinnamon years ago when she was on the road, I didn't catch that she had all this drama in her world. I don't recall meeting Barry back then either. If he's been in her life since Lotus was a child, then Lotus has to be the same age as my Junior, early forties."

Amos grabbed another roll. "Mmmm, I sure wish we could get in touch with this private investigator Barry hired. Whatever he or she found could probably clear up a lot of Cinnamon's troubles."

I smiled. "I agree. And also save us the trouble of looking. What do you think about Jared going missing? Tommy certainly had his ideas."

Amos took a drink from his tea, and then set the glass slowly on the table. "My first thought was Jared must have confronted Barry when he left the dressing room. I mean if it was me, and this big man was arguing with my grandmother, I would want to be protective and defend her."

I pushed my plate away and placed my elbows on the table. "I could see them having words. Could you tell if Jared was, as they say, packing last night? If he had a gun on him, he could have shot Barry in the heat of passion."

Amos grinned. "I couldn't tell if he was carrying or not. I wasn't really looking. I was more excited about you and Cinnamon connecting backstage." He leaned back and absently rubbed his tummy. "If he had confronted Barry and shot him, there should have been some witnesses."

I pointed my finger because I knew this. "And there should have been blood on his clothes."

Being married to a former homicide detective, Amos and I had the most interesting discussions. While I wasn't a detective, I'd watched enough *Law & Order, CSI* and other television crime shows to know shooting someone didn't come without getting some evidence sprayed back on oneself.

Amos nodded. "If he had some evidence on his clothes, they would've had good reason to take him to the police station and have him turn in his clothes. If that was the case, Cinnamon and Lotus would have to find him a lawyer. They still may need to if the detectives assigned to Barry's case want to talk to him. If the detectives catch wind that Jared's missing, that's not going to be good."

I sat back in my seat, feeling the exhaustion from the day. "Jared seemed in shock at the hospital. Maybe he witnessed Barry getting shot..." I stopped talking as a thought occurred to me. Then I leaned forward. "Amos, maybe Jared isn't hiding because he's the shooter. Suppose he saw the shooter and knows who it is?"

Amos cocked his head. "If that's the case, why not just come forward? Not unless he's protecting someone?"

I added. "Or maybe he's afraid of someone?"

The server returned with the dessert menu. While the desserts looked scrumptious, we decided to walk off the meal. Once Amos took care of the bill, I followed him out hand-in-hand toward the music. There was music everywhere, of course, because we were walking down Music Row.

I could see there was a lot of history in this area, which I loved. The magic that we'd been missing from the trip became more obvious to me as I took the time to look at the buildings we passed by. Where I was tired before, the meal and the walk energized me.

So enthralled with the views, I didn't realize my cell phone had been ringing. I stopped walking. Amos turned to watch as I pulled the phone out of my bag to peer at the screen.

When I saw Cinnamon's number, my heart skipped a beat as I wondered what news she had for us. She'd already shared some pretty good whoppers for the day.

Maybe Jared had returned home.

"Hello?" I answered cautiously, trying to keep my voice steady.

"Eugeena, it's Cinnamon." Her voice sounded far away and barely audible.

My grip tightened on the phone as worry settled in my chest. "Cinnamon, I can hardly hear you."

"I'm... I'm at the hospital," she choked out.

Panic bubbled within me, and I shot Amos a concerned glance. His brow furrowed in worry.

I squeezed my eyes shut for a moment, trying to collect my thoughts. "Are you at the same hospital as last night?"

"Yes, the ambulance took me to Nashville General."

I glanced at Amos, whose resigned expression probably matched mine, before I reassured her. "Amos and I will be there as soon as we can."

"Thank you, Eugeena," she murmured, relief clear in her tone. "I don't know who to trust anymore."

Amos's words echoed in my mind.

Suppose Cinnamon isn't totally being honest with you?

My friend's life was a complete mystery to me.

Chapter 11

I wasn't sure how we managed to be back at the hospital again. We were just here last night waiting to see if Barry would make it. He didn't. And now Cinnamon was here only hours after she admitted her fear of being next.

I wasn't family, so I had to do a lot of explaining at the nurse's desk. Finally, I pushed open the door to Cinnamon's hospital room. The smell of antiseptic and disinfectant hung heavily in the air. I approached her bed, my heart aching at the sight of her bruised face. They'd meticulously wrapped her arm in bandages, and her eyes reflected a mixture of weariness and fear as I drew closer to her.

I looked over by the bed and noticed she already had a visitor. Niecy smiled. "Oh, good. I'm so glad you could come. I've been calling Lotus so other people knew Cinnamon was in the hospital."

Cinnamon reached out to pat the young woman's hand. "Thank you for coming."

Niecy held Cinnamon's hand. "Absolutely. I'm glad you had me listed as one of your emergency contacts. You were so lucky."

I walked closer to the bed to examine Cinnamon up close. "Sistah girl, are you okay?"

Cinnamon tried to shake her head, but winced. "Everything is going so wrong, Eugeena."

I glanced over at Niecy who stood from the chair. "Here, Ms. Eugeena. Why don't you sit here? I need to go, but I wanted to make sure someone was by Cinnamon's side."

"Of course. Thank you."

Cinnamon tried to say something, but seemed to have trouble speaking. Finally she croaked, "Jared."

Niecy looked at me, and then back at Cinnamon. Her eyes were sad. "I'm sorry. I haven't been able to find him yet."

I frowned. "Did he say anything to you last night, anything that might suggest he was going to disappear?"

Niecy shook her head. "He was really scared the cops were going to bother him. Other than that, I think he was just in shock. I dropped him off at his apartment, but I don't know where he went after that. He looked exhausted to me. Don't worry I will keep trying."

I nodded. A young black man had reason to fear cops, but I wondered if there was another reason.

After Niecy left, I sat in the chair that she'd just occupied. I leaned over and asked. "Cinnamon, what on earth happened?"

Cinnamon winced as she shifted in the bed, trying to find a comfortable position. "I lost control of my car, Eugeena. I guided it out of traffic, thank the Lord. But I did so much damage."

"Thank, God, you're alright."

"Alright might be pushin' it," she replied with a weak smile. "But it could've been much worse. Eugeena," Cinnamon began hesitantly. Her voice fell to a whisper despite it only being me and her in the room. "I kept pushing the brake, but it wouldn't work. It went straight to the floor. I drove that car last week, and it was fine. Someone messed with it."

My mind raced.

Was Cinnamon telling me her brakes stopped working?

Tears ran down Cinnamon's face. "Now I'm wondering if something happened to Jared." Her bruised face showed the strain of her emotions. "I'm just so scared for him."

I'd only met the young man once, but even I was worried about him. Surely, he'd be here at the hospital with his beloved grandmother. "Has Jared been in some type of trouble? If so, are you sure that trouble hasn't followed Jared?"

Cinnamon sighed heavily, her eyes clouded with worry. "I've been pushing Jared to sing again. He used to be in his own boy band."

I could picture the young man alongside other men dancing and driving girls wild. "What happened?"

Cinnamon continued. "He's been reluctant to get back into the business since his friend died. Jared has never done drugs, but he's been around people who love the party scene a bit too much. He's just...so afraid of goin' down that same path, and I don't blame him. The music business can suck the life out of you and your dreams."

"You know when I first saw Jared, he reminded me of your brother, Charlie. Now he could sing!"

Cinnamon tried to smile, but she grimaced in pain instead. "Yes, Jared reminds me so much of my brother. It's crazy how the genes jump around in generations. Lotus looks nothing like me, but the first time I saw Jared..." Cinnamon sucked in a breath. "It's been so long, but I still miss Charlie, even after all these years."

Cinnamon's brother had been handsome, charming, and always the life of the party. "Your brother was my first crush, you know," I confessed, surprising even myself with the sudden admission. "I used to follow him around like a little puppy dog hoping he'd notice me."

Cinnamon laughed gently. "Really? I never knew that."

"Well, I wasn't exactly subtle about it," I said with a chuckle, recalling my younger self's clumsy attempts at flirtation. "But he was always kind to me, even when he didn't have to be."

"Sounds like him alright," Cinnamon agreed. "He would've loved Jared, you know. They are kind of alike. My brother got mixed up in things he shouldn't have, and it cost him his life. I just don't want Jared goin' down that same path."

"I understand." It concerned me how much Cinnamon worried about Jared. She'd just said she lost control of her car. I would have been more concerned about almost dying. With the revelation that Cinnamon's accident involved something more sinister, I steered the conversation in a different direction. "Let's focus on finding out who could be out to hurt you. What about those band members you let go?"

Cinnamon furrowed her brow. "How did you know about that?"

I didn't want to throw Niecy under the bus, so I deflected. "You wanted us to help you. Believe it or not, Amos and I have some experience getting to the truth, even when it's not pretty."

Cinnamon frowned. "Well, there was Olivia Harris. She used to be one of my background singers, but we started butting heads after a while."

"Olivia Harris? What was the issue between y'all?"

"Olivia had a strong voice and stage presence," Cinnamon said with some reluctance. "I always knew she wanted to go solo, but I never thought it would come between us like it did."

"She was on the stage the other night at the Blue Note Lounge."

Cinnamon raised an eyebrow. "You have always been smart, Eugeena. Sounds like you've been doing your homework."

I grinned. "So you think she might hold a grudge against you?"

"Maybe," Cinnamon replied hesitantly, her fingers fidgeting with the edge of her blanket. "But I don't know for sure. We don't speak to each other, but I can't imagine her hurting me. She has what she wants now–that solo career. Her husband, Jack Harris, owns the Blue Note."

"Would it be alright if I talked to Olivia, Cinnamon?" I asked cautiously, not wanting to upset her further. "I think it's important we explore all possibilities."

Cinnamon shrugged, wincing slightly from the movement. "I guess it wouldn't hurt. She probably will have a lot of nasty things to say about me. Things were... tense between us before I let her go."

"Ah, I see," I murmured. I couldn't help but feel a pang of sympathy for both women. The music business was tough enough without having to navigate personal rivalries and power struggles. Apparently, their falling out had taken a toll on Cinnamon's spirits.

"You know, Barry wouldn't have put me on the same stage and night with Olivia," Cinnamon sighed. "He always knew how to handle things like that. But Jared... Well, bless his heart, he didn't know any better when he booked the gig."

Recalling Tommy rant about not getting paid, I asked. "How are things going with the gigs? I know you found out money was missing from your bank accounts. Has this affected how you manage payments? I imagine you don't trust using that account."

"You're right. I started another bank account, one that Barry didn't have access to. I also removed him from my other accounts."

I wanted to ask Cinnamon more, but a sudden movement caught my eye. An official-looking man and woman stood at Cinnamon's hospital doorway. As they entered the room, I felt a subtle shift in the atmosphere and I immediately thought... detectives.

"Hello, Ms. Waters, I'm Detective Davis, and this is my partner, Detective Harris. We're here to ask you a few questions."

Detective Davis, the older of the two, a tall African American with graying temples, eyed me as if I were in the way.

I could take a hint. Though I really wanted to sit and find out why the detectives were there, I patted Cinnamon's hand. "I'll be right outside in the waiting room area with Amos."

I turned to take another look as the detectives flanked Cinnamon on each side of her bed. She seemed smaller, like she'd shriveled within to protect herself.

"Lord," I prayed quietly, my hands clasped together tightly, "please watch over Cinnamon and give her the strength she needs to face whatever comes next."

Chapter 12

I closed Cinnamon's hospital room door, feeling anxious about the two detectives' arrival. I had my run-ins back home with detectives and knew some of the questions coming. With Cinnamon's accident so close to Barry's death, there were bound to be some inquiries into what in the world was going on in Cinnamon's life.

I certainly wished I knew.

I joined Amos in the waiting room. He watched me as I approached, looking as tired as I felt. I was grateful for his presence, but also regretted yet another snag in our trip. At least we ate dinner and did a little sightseeing before Cinnamon's call.

I sat in the stiff-backed chair next to him. The chair next to Cinnamon's bed had been more tolerable. Amos touched my hand, and I relished the warmth and comfort.

"You alright?"

"Detectives showed up to talk to Cinnamon," I told him, my voice cracking just a little. "She thinks someone messed with her car."

Worry lines deepened on Amos's forehead. "So someone physically tried to hurt her. This is getting serious. First Barry and now her. She was right. The person behind those threats is escalating. I hope Cinnamon shares everything with the detectives. They have to investigate."

"I hope she doesn't hold back. But her and Lotus seemed to lack confidence in the police for a reason. Like you said earlier, she's not being completely honest with us either."

Something, or rather someone, caught my eye from across the waiting room. A man appeared to lurk around the waiting room entrance. And he kept looking toward Cinnamon's door.

I leaned closer to Amos. "Why does that man look suspicious to me?"

Amos's eyes followed my line of sight. A wiry man with gray around his temples shifted his weight nervously from one foot to the other. A large camera slung around his neck. Something about his hair didn't look right. The middle was too black. I suspected the black tuft of hair was more of a toupee. Or either he'd been fooled by some hair growth for men concoction. He was talking on the phone to someone, but I couldn't make out his conversation from across the room.

"Looks like we got ourselves a reporter," Amos muttered. "Paparazzi must've caught wind of Cinnamon's accident. It was bound to happen, especially since the media is covering Barry's shooting. It's known or will be known of her association with him."

I wanted to run the man off. A reporter was the last thing Cinnamon needed right now. The hospital doors slid open and Lotus stepped through. She headed straight to the nurses' station.

When we saw Lotus yesterday, her elegance struck me. Today was no different. She pulled off a bright white pantsuit paired with white sandal heels. Her hair was high on her head in a bun. Despite her mother being in the hospital and her son still missing, Lotus Waters appeared put together. Recalling yesterday's tense argument, I was glad she showed up to support her mother.

Lotus turned from the nurses' station, her eyes flitting around the waiting room. I didn't know if she saw or recognized us, but her eyes locked on the man with the camera. To my surprise, she strode toward him with determination in her every step.

Good! She should run him out of this hospital.

My hope that Lotus would run the reporter off faded as I watched them interact. She spoke in a quiet tone with him, her expression guarded. The surrounding air seemed electrified, and I held my breath, waiting for the outcome. I glanced at Amos, who also watched the exchange with interest.

"Can you believe this?" I whispered. "Lotus is actually talking to the reporter."

Amos replied, his brow furrowed with concern. "But why?"

"Lord only knows." Worry pricked at the base of my neck. Just like I didn't really know my friend, I didn't know a thing about her daughter either.

"Maybe she's trying to set the record straight," Amos suggested. "You know how these reporters can twist things around. Maybe Lotus wants to make sure he gets the facts right. She's probably wasting her time, though."

"I agree. That man came here to dig up some dirt."

Cinnamon's hospital room door swung open, and the two detectives who had been questioning her stepped out. Their expressions betrayed nothing of the conversation that had just taken place behind closed doors. They stood in the hall for a few seconds before leaving in the opposite direction of the waiting room.

I hesitated before returning to Cinnamon's room. While I was eager to know what happened, I also kept my eye on Lotus. She was still talking to the reporter, whose smile widened the entire time they talked. I didn't have long to observe Lotus because she and the reporter began walking down the hallway toward the elevators. They were right behind the detectives.

"What is going on?" I knew I had to look nosy, stretching my neck to see these folks.

Amos stood, "I don't know, but I think I will take a stroll. You check on Cinnamon and I will see what I can find out."

I lifted my tired body up off the chair and watched Amos walk briskly down the hallway. He arrived just in time to get on the elevator with the detectives. I frowned because Lotus and the reporter didn't get on the elevator.

What could they be talking about? And in such a public place.

No sense in worrying about it. I opened the door and stepped inside Cinnamon's hospital room. The door closed behind me with a soft click, shutting out the noise at the nearby nurses' station.

Cinnamon lay in her hospital bed, her eyes closed as if in a peaceful slumber. She looked so vulnerable, almost nothing at all like the vivacious singer who performed onstage last night.

Who knew that she would switch roles with Barry, except I very much wanted her to stay alive.

"Hey, Cinnamon." I whispered. "I'm back."

Her eyes fluttered open, her face grim.

I sat back in the chair next to her bed. "How did things go? You look worn out."

Cinnamon moved her head slightly against the pillow as if it was too heavy to lift. "I'm exhausted. The detectives are still checking things out, but it looks like... like my brake line had been cut."

My heart nearly skipped a beat at her words. Someone *had* deliberately tried to harm her. The thought sent chills down my spine. "Honey, how could that happen? Where have you been keeping your car?"

Cinnamon shook her head. "At home in the garage. I don't drive that often. Jared drives me everywhere."

"He drives you around using your car?"

She nodded. "Yes, that's correct."

"Is that a part of the manager's job, and I'm asking because I wonder if that was something Barry did, too?"

Cinnamon didn't answer right away. Finally, she responded. "Barry helped me pick out the car years ago. It was not the first car he helped me with, but he persuaded me to upgrade to a

Mercedes. For the longest time, I wouldn't get a luxury car like that, but he convinced me I'd earned it. He told me it was a safe car to drive too. Barry went above and beyond, often helping me schedule maintenance." She sighed and looked up at the ceiling. "You know I've never been married, but I always had some man like Barry or Jared taking care of my car. They'd even fill my gas tank for me. I guess I really am a diva like Lotus has been telling me."

I frowned because Cinnamon's relationship with Barry was far beyond him being her manager. He really cared for her, which made me wonder why didn't they get married.

Instead of blurting what was really on my mind, I said, "You're blessed. Most single women struggle on their own. Has any maintenance been done on your car recently?"

In the back of my mind, I recalled a conversation yesterday at Niecy's salon. She'd mentioned Tommy was a mechanic. I did not know why he would harm Cinnamon, though. She was the main act, bringing in the audience for the gigs. He got paid because of her.

"No, well, I don't know. In the last few months, Jared used it more than me. He didn't say anything was wrong with the car. He would have mentioned it to me."

It made me wary that so many things led back to Jared. I sensed from the brief time I saw them together that in some ways Jared was closer to Cinnamon than his mother.

I switched gears, not wanting to upset Cinnamon about her grandson. "Did you tell the detectives about the threats?"

Cinnamon sighed. "I told them everything. But so far, they ain't got much to go on. They asked if I had recent conflicts with anyone."

Not wanting to step in the detective's way, I was curious to know the answer to that question as well. "Is there anyone you can think of who might be upset with you?" I inquired carefully. "Besides Olivia Harris."

Cinnamon hesitated, then bit her lip. "Well, there is Nate Parker," she admitted. "The guitarist in my band. He was pretty angry when I fired Olivia, but that's just 'cause he has always been in love with her. He's never been in Olivia's league. She likes her men with money, which Nate never has enough of."

I thought *maybe that's why she married the owner of the Blue Note Lounge.*

"Eugeena, I know this is going to sound foolish. I should be more concerned with my safety, but Jared is still missing. It's not looking good for him."

I cocked my head to the side. "Were the detectives asking about Jared?"

"They were lookin' for him," Cinnamon's voice hitched in her throat as she tried to hold back a cry. "Oh, Eugeena. He was the last person seen talking to Barry before... Well, before everything happened. So he's a person of interest, they say. But that's not all of it. They had the nerve to hint that Jared might have had something to do with my brakes. He's my grandson, for heaven's sake!"

Cinnamon just said her grandson used her car all the time. I didn't want to think anything bad about the young man, but he had access to her.

"Has he ever worked on a car?"

Cinnamon balked at my question. "Jared knows nothing about cars."

"Okay, but does he know how to handle a gun? You need to think like the detectives. These are questions they are going to ask and investigate. With Jared not being available, what are some ways to prove them wrong about him?"

Cinnamon made a face as if she smelled something rotten. She opened her mouth to respond, but Lotus walked into the room, an uneasy expression on her face. "What y'all talkin' about?" she asked, eyeing us both.

"Detectives were here," Cinnamon explained quickly. "They're thinking someone cut my brake line. And Eugeena's asking about Jared and guns, but of course, he doesn't know how to use one."

Lotus's eyes widened, and she looked at me with something akin to fear. "Jared knows how to handle a gun. We used to go to the shootin' range together when he was younger." She hesitated, then added, "I had a guy I dated who stalked me for a while."

I know my face must have looked as stricken as Cinnamon's. We both stared at Lotus for a few seconds, stunned.

Her voice, barely audible, Cinnamon said, "I had no idea."

About the fact her daughter learned how to shoot, or that she had a stalker? Both revelations had me blown me away. But this new information raised my suspicions about Jared even more.

"You realize if he knows how to handle a gun, and if the bullets from his gun are a match to the bullet that killed Barry, he's more than a person of interest. He's a prime suspect."

Cinnamon gasped. "Lotus, where is he? You have to know where he is."

Lotus lashed out. "I don't know where he could be." She threw her hands in the air. "I don't even feel like I know him anymore. Most of the people I tried to call today haven't seen or talked to Jared in months. He's been spending more time with the great Cinnamon Waters than me."

With only the sounds of the machine humming and beeping, the hospital room grew quiet. These two women were in a constant tug of war. It was obvious Lotus resented her mother's career. I wondered if Jared felt trapped in the middle. Both of them fiercely protected him, which as the mother of two sons I could relate. But it felt like there was something else going on.

Who knew, maybe Jared went missing to avoid these confrontations between his mother and grandmother. Barry was obviously someone special to the Waters family. Conflicts often grew worse after a loved one died.

Something occurred to me that Lotus had said earlier. "You said Jared called you last night. What exactly did he say?"

Lotus looked at me like she really didn't want to answer me, but then her face softened and tears flooded her eyes. "You think he shot Barry?"

"No, I don't. But he might have said something to you that provides some clues to where he went."

Lotus shook her head. "I've thought about nothing else. Like I said earlier, he was crying so hard I could barely make out what he was saying. He said something about Barry getting shot and that he needed help. I asked him where he was, but all he would say is that it didn't matter, that all that mattered was that Barry survived. He said he had to go and hung up before I could ask any more questions."

I scooted forward in the chair. "Wait, he said that *he* needed help. Help with what?"

Lotus drew her shoulders up, and then sagged in defeat. "I don't know. Maybe I misheard him."

Cinnamon said. "No, I could see him asking for help. He saw Barry get shot. Barry and I argued. The detective said witnesses saw Jared and Barry arguing. I'm sure he was telling Barry to stay away from me." She turned to me. "But the police have no evidence Jared had a gun on him or that he shot Barry. Even if he knows how to shoot, he wouldn't walk around with a gun. At least I've never noticed one on him."

Lotus grew quiet.

I asked, "Lotus, would he carry for protection? It's not uncommon for young men to gravitate toward a weapon for security. You know, back home, we had a bad crime wave one year. My son Cedric told me he got a license to carry because he worked long hours at the hospital and never knew what to expect late at night or early morning hours."

Lotus glanced at her mother. "Jared had been having trouble with someone. But I think that's all settled down. Mom, I don't see him carrying while he was working at your gig. Besides, if people saw Jared talking with Barry, then someone should have seen him pull the trigger."

I nodded. There definitely should have been witnesses. But people clammed up and didn't want to be involved in the legal process of participating in a trial.

Also, only guilty people ran and hide.

Either way, things were certainly not looking good for Jared.

Chapter 13

It was late when Amos and I trudged back into our hotel room. While the room was comfortable, I started experiencing a bit of homesickness. I loved that Amos and I had finally gotten away, but I also missed our daily routines back home. Sitting around in the kitchen or hanging out in our rocking chairs on the front porch were moments of peace we had together.

Amos had poured so much into this trip, he seemed deflated more so than I'd ever seen him. It had been a long day, starting with breakfast and the possibility of enjoying the city we had selected to experience together. But from the moment Cinnamon called to inform us of Barry's death, the day had gone downhill with a few highlights. Amos had his first pedicure, and we'd enjoyed a meal together before getting sucked back into Cinnamon's whirlwind of drama and chaotic relationships.

After a hot shower, I rubbed the steam from the mirror and stared at my face. They say black don't crack, and mostly that's true. But tonight I looked tired, and Lord knows I felt tired. It was a good thing we had another few days left here in Nashville before we traveled around to other parts of the state next week.

This was supposed to be a leisurely trip. A romantic trip. The first trip that I had taken in years. Amos and I left to take a break from this kind of stuff back home. As much as I wanted to help Cinnamon, I also wanted our time back. But I knew we might be stuck until something happened. I prayed that there would be no more tragedies.

I cracked open the bathroom door to find Amos sitting up in bed, his eyes half-closed. The large flat screen television on the opposite wall played softly in the background. It appeared to be the news which, despite my melancholy mood, I was curious to hear. This was Cinnamon's city and as a local celebrity, her car crash would not go unnoticed.

With the focus on Jared at the hospital, I didn't have time to question Lotus about her conversation with the reporter. I didn't see any reason to mention the incident to Cinnamon either. The mother and daughter relationship was already on rocky ground.

I unwrapped my bathrobe from around my pale pink silk nightie. My skin shivered slightly, immediately missing the warmth of the soft fabric. I scrambled under the cool plush duvet, which invited a good night's sleep. I had so much going on in my mind I wondered if I could truly sleep well tonight.

I leaned over to Amos, pressing a gentle kiss to his cheek. We had returned to the hotel in an unusual silence. At least unusual for me. I wanted to talk about all I learned, but I knew Amos needed to process quietly, and I'd learned to honor his needs.

But not for the first time on this trip, I wanted to make sure he wasn't upset with me. I patted his hand. "Thank you for being supportive about Cinnamon again."

His deep chuckle warmed me, easing some of my nervousness. He turned to face me. "We can't just turn our backs on her now, can we?"

"No, we can't."

Amos sighed heavily. "You know, Eugeena, I've been thinking... I can't help but feel responsible for putting us in this mess. It was my idea to treat you to Cinnamon's concert during our honeymoon trip."

"Amos, honey," I reached over and gave his hand a reassuring squeeze. "You didn't know any of this was going to happen. It appears our mission at this stage of our lives involves helping people who need it. Location doesn't seem to be a factor. So now that we got that out of the way, did you find out anything on your stroll?"

Amos smirked. "I introduced myself to the detectives. They weren't impressed with my out-of-town retired detective spiel, but then again, that wasn't my reason for following them down the elevator. Detective Quincy Davis and Detective Hannah Wilson now know that Cinnamon has some former law enforcement in her corner. They may not have appreciated my introduction, but cops always check around to find out about someone in their jurisdiction. When I was on the force, I sure did. Also, one of my buddies worked on an FBI task force a few years ago on a case here in Tennessee. I asked him for a favor."

I cocked my head. "Look at you! I was worried that you were really regretting this trip. I'm glad you're checking to make sure they take Cinnamon's threats seriously."

"Well, it concerned me earlier today when she claimed she'd shared those threats with the police and they did nothing. It also bothered me that Barry was accused of stealing her money, but yet we heard nothing about charges against him. And why was he there at the Blue Note Lounge still having access to Cinnamon? She should have called security as soon as he entered her dressing room."

Amos had brought up some valid points. "Maybe she did. Or maybe she really wanted to hear him out. I feel like she was in love with him at one time. Maybe she still is. Also, remember, she thought he could have been threatening her. He was a big, intimidating man. Cinnamon could have been scared of him."

Amos continued talking as if a lid had popped open on his thoughts. "But everyone so far has said what a good guy he was. No one believed he would steal from Cinnamon. Why did she believe it so much? So many things make little sense. I know the detectives weren't shy about asking me about Jared. I had to tell them I only met him for the first time two nights ago."

"You know, Lotus confirmed Jared knows how to use a gun." I filled him in on the rest of the conversation with Lotus and Cinnamon.

Amos whistled. "So, if Jared owns the gun that matches the bullets in Barry's body, or if they found the gun in or around that parking lot," Amos shook his head, "it's going to be a manhunt if that boy doesn't show up. I sure would like to get my hands on that report to figure out the caliber of gun and the suspect's distance from the victim. He may not have gotten blood spatter on his clothes, but there would be gun residue on his hands for sure if he fired a weapon."

I folded the duvet over my chest, feeling my exhaustion return. "Would the police have collected anything from him after they interviewed him? They are working on a theory that he was the last person seen talking to Barry before he was shot."

Amos frowned. "I saw the deputy on the scene take Jared's statement, but they still would have wanted him to come in for further questioning so he could sign the statement."

"But he went missing instead." Something else bothered me and I shifted in the bed to turn on my side so I could face Amos more. "You know Jared should have been at the hospital with his grandmother. From everything we've heard, he's extremely close to Cinnamon. I hate to say it, but that young man is looking way too guilty."

Amos held my gaze. "You're right, Eugeena. Here's another theory. Maybe Jared is more interested in getting his hands on his grandmother's money than he is in her well-being. I wouldn't be surprised if everything with Barry was a setup."

"We don't know the young man, but you think he had enough gumption to steal from Cinnamon?" I thought about it. "When Cinnamon says money was stolen from her, she didn't really say how it was stolen. These days, most payments are electronic transactions. I suppose a person with the right skill set could interfere with a transaction."

Amos nodded. "Absolutely. And it wouldn't take much for Jared to get access to his grandmother's account numbers. Most folks keep those things lying around in their house."

The implications that this young man did something this horrible to his own grandmother still didn't sit right with me. "Jared would certainly have a motive to shoot Barry. But I'm not feeling that theory. If the young man was responsible for Barry's death, I would think he did it to protect his grandmother. He reminded me of how my sons would react when their protective mode is activated."

In the back of my mind, it almost seemed too obvious that it was Jared. Although both Cinnamon and Lotus were worried about the young man, neither one had been forthcoming. But it sounded like Jared had run into some trouble before. Lotus didn't confirm, but in so many words she admitted Jared had a gun and he carried.

Then, I remembered Cinnamon mentioned in her last conversation with Barry that he'd hired a private detective. In fact, if Barry hadn't been shot, he would have been at Cinnamon's house the next day to explain what he'd found.

Who knew about him reaching out to a private detective?

Once again, that could have been something Jared easily overheard.

I noticed Amos lifting his torso away from the pillows, his eyes were intense as he stared at the television. He grabbed the remote and raised the volume. Curious about what had his attention, I peeked over the duvet. Then I sat straight up.

The news anchor talked while several images were displayed of a dark vehicle. I immediately assumed that it was Cinnamon's Mercedes. I hadn't realized she'd smashed the car into the side of a building. The front end had crumpled like an accordion.

"Praise the Lord," I whispered. "Cinnamon survived that!"

The anchorwoman, her voice somber, detailed the events of the day. "Famous singer Cinnamon Waters crashed her vehicle into a local store earlier today causing extensive damage. The owners are understandably upset and seeking compensation."

"According to witnesses," the anchor continued, "Ms. Waters appeared to have lost control of her car at the time of the accident. It's unclear what led to the crash, but authorities are investigating."

I sputtered. "Oh no! This is so much worse. Cinnamon didn't mention crashing into a store. I wonder if she even remembers what really happened."

Just then, the anchorwoman shifted gears, her tone growing even graver. "In related news, Barry Jenkins, former manager of Cinnamon Waters, was shot on Monday evening behind the Blue Note Lounge. The circumstances of the incident remain unclear, and we now turn to our correspondent, Ben Taylor for more information."

The screen flickered as the news segment transitioned to a familiar face, and I gasped. "Amos, that's the reporter we saw at the hospital!"

Amos narrowed his eyes. "I knew it."

"Earlier today, Cinnamon Waters was involved in a car accident when her vehicle crashed into a local store," Taylor began, looking as solemn and professional as he could. At least he'd taken some gel or something and smoothed that black tuft of hair back away from his face. "Sources close to the singer say she has been unwell for some time now, which may have played a role in the crash."

"Unwell?" I repeated.

Is that what Lotus told the reporter? And was it true?

I felt a surge of anger at this Ben Taylor. The way he showed up at the hospital to get a story. I witnessed how fragile Lotus's relationship was with her mother. There wasn't anything that could be done about the past. It was often best to come to terms with past issues and move forward in the present. That appeared to be what Cinnamon had tried to do. Lotus shouldn't have allowed Cinnamon's personal struggles to be offered for the masses to consume.

I huffed, diving back under the covers. "They shouldn't be broadcasting Cinnamon's private life like this."

"Unfortunately, Eugeena, that's how the news works these days," Amos sighed, shaking his head. "It's all about getting the most sensational story regardless of who it hurts."

"I know. But do you really think Cinnamon is unwell?"

"I think something is affecting her. She's been pushing people away."

I sighed. "How about tomorrow we start by visiting the Blue Note Lounge and talk to Olivia Harris? She's known Cinnamon for years and might have some insight into what's really going on."

"Sounds like a plan," Amos agreed. "At least we know the food is good."

Despite the gravity of our situation, I couldn't help but chuckle at my husband's attempt to lighten the mood. "You and your fried chicken, Amos. Even if our honeymoon isn't going exactly as planned, there's no one else I'd rather spend this time with than you."

He looked at me and smiled, the wrinkles around his eyes deepening. "Me neither, Eugeena."

As the television screen continued to flicker, casting eerie shadows across our hotel room, I snuggled down under the covers and closer to Amos. I closed my eyes and focused on the steady rhythm of Amos's heartbeat, allowing it to lull me into a state of relaxation. A small part of me couldn't help but worry about what we would uncover in the coming days.

Chapter 14

Amos and I stepped through the double doors of the Blue Note Lounge. Even on a late Wednesday afternoon, the lounge was dimly lit. Sunlight beamed through a few windows, but most of them had light filtering shades pulled low. A low hum of conversations mixed with the clinking of glasses provided the backdrop to the sultry music emanating from the stage. Despite the shooting the other night, people still visited for happy hour.

As we grabbed a table near the stage, the woman we wanted to talk to crooned out a ballad I didn't recognize. Olivia Harris's sweet voice wrapped around every syllable like honey dripping off a spoon. Applause erupted all around us as she hit the final note of the song. When the applause died down, Olivia stepped off the stage, her face flushed with the glow of her performance. Amos and I exchanged glances before rising from our chairs.

"Ms. Harris?" I called out gently, careful not to startle her.

Olivia turned around, her eyes meeting mine with curiosity and a touch of apprehension. I was sure she probably had fans approach her all the time.

"Ms. Harris, I'm Eugeena Patterson-Jones and this is my husband, Amos. We're old friends of Cinnamon Waters. We wondered if you had some time to talk to us?"

Olivia's eyes widened in surprise as she observed us. "It's an honor to meet you both. I'm not sure what you want to talk about, but I don't sing with Cinny anymore."

I noticed Olivia referred to Cinnamon by her nickname too.

"I know. That's why I wanted to talk to you. It seems something has been going on with Cinnamon and it's only getting worse, especially with Barry's death. We sure would appreciate any insights you could offer."

Olivia's eyes filled with pain and regret, as if we'd cracked open a fresh wound. "I have been concerned about Cinny for a while now. It hurt me to see our twenty plus year friendship go up in dust. I know she's hurting right now after Barry's death. They were close for so many years. We all were close. Let's get you a table."

We followed Olivia over to a table in a cozy corner away from the crowd. Olivia beckoned a server to come over. "Why don't y'all get something from the menu? Our hot fried chicken is fantastic. It's on the house."

I peeked over at Amos, who couldn't wipe that grin off his face if he tried.

It didn't take long after ordering for the server to return with steaming plates of food. We were halfway through our meal before Olivia returned to our table. She'd changed out of her stage clothes, looking casual but elegant in a jumpsuit. Apprehension still hung around her face.

"Where should I start?" she asked.

"It's up to you. We already talked to Cinnamon. She requested our help."

Olivia stared at me. "You must be really special. Cinny doesn't ask for help."

"We were childhood friends back in Charleston, South Carolina. We grew up out in the country and were always at each other's houses."

Olivia cocked her head. "Eugeena. She talked about you sometimes. That was a special time for her. And, I know she lost a brother, her only sibling."

That warmed me that Cinnamon mentioned our friendship to Olivia. "That's right."

Olivia gave us a small smile. "I'm glad that you stayed friends all these years. It pains me to think about our lost friendship. We had some good times together."

I responded, "Maybe we can figure out what's going on. We need to fast because too many things are happening."

Olivia's face grew somber. "I know about the car crash. It's all over the news. I feel bad for her. Cinny has always been a wonderful soul. We all have our moments when life just isn't fair. The past year has been like that for her."

Amos pushed his plate back, looking full and ready to get into the conversation. "So everything started about a year ago."

Olivia crossed her arms and looked off into the distance. "Yes. I guess so now that you mentioned it. It started with her grandson."

"Jared?" I exchanged a glance with Amos. "What about him?"

"Well, he's quite the talent. He has a beautiful singing voice. His mama does too. But Lotus had no interest in the music business. She's more into art. If you haven't visited Lotus's art gallery, you should. She has some beautiful pieces in there that she painted herself."

"I heard Cinnamon helped get the art gallery started."

Olivia nodded. "Cinny was on the road so much when Lotus was young. By the time Lotus was a teenager, they just didn't get along. Things smoothed out for them when Lotus had Jared. He's Cinnamon's pride and joy. Where she couldn't be there for Lotus, Cinnamon supported her grandson. Jared is just like his grandmother. You know he was in a boy band, him and three other guys. Everyone thought they were going to blow up and get big. They even had a few music labels seriously considering them."

"What happened?" I asked. "How did Jared go from a boy band to replacing Barry as Cinnamon's manager?"

Olivia shook her head. "That part about how Jared became her manager is a puzzle to me. He's too young and inexperienced. But I know why Cinny did it. She was trying to save him. Save his very soul as she described it."

I frowned. "Something bad happened."

"Yeah, one member of his boy band always had a little more ego than the rest. Loved the girls, loved to party and was into drugs. He got ahold of some bad heroin laced with fentanyl. He overdosed. Jared found his friend and tried to get him help, but it was too late. For a while, the cops were looking at Jared. Somehow they got it in their head that Jared supplied the drugs, but Jared never touched that kind of stuff. He barely drinks alcohol. The police finally left him alone, but he hasn't been the same."

I twisted my hands together. Poor Jared! Now I understood why his mother and grandmother tried to protect him. He'd been traumatized twice. Finding his bandmate dead and then being falsely accused.

Amos had been listening intently. "That was a big stretch to accuse him of drug dealing. Where do you think the idea came from?"

Olivia shrugged. "Someone set him up. He's always been smart and a bit awkward. Definitely an easy target. His mother put him in private school for a reason. Other students bullied him in school."

"Mmmm," I commented. "He really takes after his uncle Charlie."

"Cinny's brother?" Olivia inquired. "She used to say that too. I also think that's why she's super protective of him."

"The rumors were Charlie got killed messing around with someone who was supposed to be a friend. Bubba Samson. The sad thing was everyone else knew Bubba was always up to no good. Drinking hard liquor despite being underage. Charlie admired Bubba and always tried to see the good in people. One night, a brawl broke out after a game with a rival school. The ringleader was guess who?"

Olivia nodded. "Bubba."

I shook my head. The loss was just as painful as it was close to five decades ago. "Charlie got stabbed, and he bled out. Bubba left him there, and didn't even come to the funeral."

Amos shook his head. "Wow, that's messed up. I didn't know it all went down like that."

I nodded. "That was a big deal. Cinnamon and her family moved away by the next school year. They were so good and generous. I feel bad that all this is happening in Cinnamon's life now. It might get a little better if Jared would just show up."

Olivia's eyes widened. "Jared is missing. When? He was here the night Barry died. Jack, that's my husband, told me Jared was upset with how Barry started an argument with Cinny. Jack tried to stop Barry from going back there, but Barry was determined to speak to her after her show."

"Did anyone see Jared talking to Barry?"

Olivia shook her head. "No, I was in my dressing room when all that went down. I heard the shots, but Jack came to my door and told me to sit still. I didn't know if someone was shooting up the place or not. When I left, I saw everyone had gone outside. That's when I found out what happened."

Amos asked, "So Jack was trying to keep Barry away from Ms. Waters? I guess you all heard that she fired him as her manager."

Olivia rubbed her temples as if to stave off a bad headache. "Everyone heard that news. She fired him during her birthday party. She had a big cookout at her house. I used to go to those before me and her had a falling out. Good food, good music and a lot of celebrities, some old and others new to the business. The next day on social media, people were all talking about how she'd fired Barry for betraying her trust."

"Are you kidding?" I couldn't believe what I was hearing. I frequent social media a few times a week, but I hadn't seen anything.

Olivia continued picking up a napkin and using it like a fan near her face. "Yes, the arguments between Barry and Cinny were world famous in circles around here. Barry... What can I say about Barry? He was a bit of a hustler. You have to be in this business. He made sure Cinny got the best gigs, but he also took care of the band, too."

I inquired. "So Barry and Cinnamon were a couple?"

Olivia smirked. "Oh, they were on and off. Hot and heavy one minute, cold as ice the next. I can tell you when they were on, everything was good with the band. Expect smooth sailing. But when Barry did something that Cinnamon didn't like, everyone knew it. Cinnamon would never admit it, but Barry was the love of her life. The problem was Barry's eyes strayed too much for Cinnamon."

Amos commented. "He was a player too?"

Olivia crossed her arms. "Bless his soul. He was a good-looking man, and he knew it. But even though he messed up sometimes, Cinny was the one he really wanted."

I drank some tea, trying to get my thoughts together. So far, Olivia had been open, filling in some details that we'd only learned about in the past few days.

But there was something I really wanted to know.

Did Olivia hold a grudge? Would she be the one threatening Cinnamon? Olivia certainly knew many intimate details about Cinnamon's life. Might as well come right out and ask. I placed my glass on the table, the remaining ice clinking against the glass. "So what happened between you and Cinnamon?"

Olivia looked off into the distance for a few seconds like she needed to collect her thoughts. Her eyes had grown weary, and her face drooped, making me think she was older than I originally thought. Or maybe the loss of friendship with Cinnamon had taken a toll on her.

Finally she responded, "At the time, it could have been the stress with Jared, but out of the blue, Cinny seemed paranoid.

About everything. I knew she was worried, but when she suddenly started accusing me of stealing gigs from her and saying I was trying to sabotage her career, I couldn't take it. Sure, I had my career on the side, but I'd been a backup singer for her most of her career. I enjoyed our friendship, and the energy that Cinny brought to the stage was like no one else."

"I'm sorry. Sometimes disagreements can blow up."

Olivia shook her head. "No, it was more than that. We were like sisters, and then one day, everything changed. I would never hurt her, and she always told me it was fine for me to do my own gigs. In fact, she supported me. But then, she started seeing me as some threat."

As Olivia spoke to us, a shadow fell over our table.

Looking up, an older man stood by our table. Despite the warm temperatures outside, he wore a crisp black suit paired with a red bowtie and a concerned expression. I remembered him onstage on Monday night. He'd been the emcee. I guessed by the way the man placed his hands on Olivia's shoulders that this was Jack Harris. Her husband and the owner of Blue Note Lounge.

"Is everything all right?" Jack asked, his dark eyes flicking between Olivia and us.

"Jack," Olivia grabbed her husband's hand and patted it reassuringly, "Meet Eugeena and Amos. They're Cinnamon's friends."

Jack raised a bushy eyebrow. "Ms. Waters could use some friends right now. She has a lot going on. It's a shame about Barry. He was a fine gentleman. I still can't believe someone shot him. And had the nerve to do it at this fine establishment."

Amos asked. "Looks like the cops let you open back up pretty quickly."

Jack raised an eyebrow. "Not without a lot of fussing from me. I've been in this town my whole life and I know a few people, like the mayor and the police chief."

Oh my! This man was not one to mess with.

Jack sat down at our table. He took a handkerchief out of his jacket pocket and wiped his forehead, or rather, his head. Like Amos, Jack sported a shiny round bald head. "We had detectives in here earlier, still prowling around."

Amos nodded. "A Detective Davis and Detective Harris?"

Jack raised an eyebrow. "You met them?"

I added, "They came to see Cinnamon at the hospital."

"Ah, I see." Jack nodded. "I can imagine they wanted to talk to her and that grandson of hers. Everyone backstage heard the argument between Cinnamon and Barry. I tried to stop him from going back there, but he was determined."

That's what his wife told us too. I asked, "Did you know Barry well?"

"Oh, yeah. I knew him when he was a youngster. Barry could play a mean piano when he wanted, but he seemed to like the business side of things. I know it hurt him when Cinnamon accused him of stealing. Made little sense to me. Barry had never been a man who hurt for money."

My thoughts churned. "Did Barry ever mention anything going on with Cinnamon to either of you? Maybe something that he was concerned about."

Jack looked at Olivia, and she held his gaze. He patted his wife's hand. "Barry admitted to me one time he thought Cinnamon seemed unwell, that she accused people of things more and more. It bothered him because it seemed so sudden. She's not a typical diva, but even I noticed that her personality seemed to change."

I shook my head. "What could have caused such a drastic change in her behavior? Maybe there is something going on with her health wise."

Of course that wouldn't explain someone cutting her brakes, sending her threats or Barry's shooting.

Jack leaned forward in his chair. "I always felt like someone was manipulating her somehow."

I whipped my head around because that would have never occurred to me. "Who would do that?"

Olivia rubbed her brow. "I hate to say this, but sometimes the people closest to you can do you the most harm."

Since Amos and I had just talked about this last night, I blurted out, "Jared?"

Olivia's eyes widened. "No, not Jared. He would never hurt Cinny." She straightened in her chair, her eyes hard. "But that daughter of hers. Cinny has tried to make things up to that girl, but Lotus's resentfulness borders on hatred."

I recalled the tension between mother and daughter. There definitely was a level of pent up resentfulness coming from Lotus. Then there was Lotus talking to the reporter at the hospital. And she also wasn't too surprised about the threatening letters.

Barry had told Cinnamon someone close to her couldn't be trusted. We, and the police, had been focusing on Jared, and him missing in action had fueled our theories.

But maybe we'd been looking at the wrong relative.

Chapter 15

After talking with Olivia and Jack, we stayed and enjoyed another show at the Blue Note Lounge. Before we left, Jack showed us an area that I hadn't noticed on Monday when we visited the Blue Note Lounge. I knew Cinnamon had made this town her home, but this town, or at least this place, loved Cinnamon Waters.

Sistah had a whole wall dedicated to her career and life. It looked like a little shrine or something.

"Who pulled this all together?" I asked.

Olivia appeared sheepish, and then explained. "Jack and I have been dating on and off for a long time. He'd been a bachelor for so long I concluded he didn't care for marriage. He opened up this place about seven years ago. The opening was around Cinnamon's birthday. Jack has always been a fan, and we both believe in giving people their flowers while living. So I assembled all the photos I'd collected over the years."

It was an amazing collection. I took a snapshot of every framed photo, not even sure why. I gathered from our talk that Olivia seemed like she had been a really good friend to Cinnamon. I hoped there was something I could do to bring these two women back together.

Amos had fallen asleep pretty quickly, deciding he didn't want to watch the news. I didn't blame him. The information Jack and Olivia shared had been enlightening. And disturbing too. While Amos snored softly beside me, I could not drift off to sleep as easily. So I took out my phone and pulled up the collection of photos from the infamous Cinnamon Waters wall.

I was grateful for the time alone with my thoughts. I realized over the past few days how much I didn't know about my childhood friend's life. It made me a tad bit homesick for my family. I had differences with my two sons and daughter over the years, but it was a part of the parent-child relationship. I had no doubts about my children's love for me and they knew I would move mountains if I could for them.

Could Lotus, or even her son, harbor enough hatred against Cinnamon to cause her harm? I didn't want to believe that.

I swiped through the photos, some dating back to a young, vibrant Cinnamon holding Lotus while onstage. Cinnamon's eyes glistened with love toward her daughter, who appeared around the age of two or three. Lotus smiled, showing off chubby cheeks and a dimple as she reached toward her mother.

Many other photos included Cinnamon onstage singing solo and some with her band. Cinnamon stood in the middle of one photo with two women, one on each side of her. I recognized a younger version of Olivia, but didn't recognize the other woman. Something about her face looked familiar, though. I'd taken my bifocals off and laid them on the nightstand. Not wanting to put them back on, I squinted to read the caption. The other woman's name was Diana Hemingway.

Oh, that must have been Niecy's mom. Now I could see the resemblance in the nose structure and the eyes.

Another photo showed Cinnamon standing next to Barry Jenkins. Over the past few days, I'd seen various pictures of the man on the news and social media, but this one was different. I could tell they'd taken this picture when their relationship had been great as Olivia explained to us earlier.

Barry's arms hung around Cinnamon's shoulders, and her arms wrapped around his waist. There was a significant height difference between them, but the camera didn't lie. They gazed at each other as if they weren't even aware of the person taking the picture. This was a man that my friend had loved. She'd never fully trusted her heart to marry him, though. But that was because Barry may have enjoyed being a bachelor. He had to have feelings for her too, since he'd been determined to clear his name.

Really, their tumultuous relationship sounded like most other celebrities who were in show business. I felt bad for Cinnamon, for that girl I knew growing up. We'd talked many times as young girls, and then later as teens about dreams of becoming someone's wife. Back in my day, family encouraged young women to find a good husband and get married. Of course, both Cinnamon and I became mothers way too young. My father insisted with an actual shotgun that Ralph Patterson marry me. Our marriage wasn't easy, but we had three children and successful careers before Ralph left this earth.

I glanced over at Amos as he slept. A wave of gratitude and love washed over me. Senior citizenship had been very humbling and, at one time, lonely. God enabled Amos and my paths to cross and eventually come together as a couple for the final phase of our lives.

I wanted the same for my friend.

But someone was purposely rocking her world.

On Thursday, we started our fourth day in Nashville a little later than usual. Amos and I agreed it was time to talk to Lotus alone, but decided we would approach her in a public setting. We arrived at a small brick building with double glass doors. The elegant lettering on the door displayed "Lotus Fine Art Gallery."

Amos opened the doors, and we walked into the cool air. Soft, soothing jazz melodies played in the background creating a serene atmosphere. We hadn't seen any artwork yet, but I could tell this was a classy place.

"Good afternoon," a warm voice greeted us as we stepped further into the space. A young woman with a short bob smiled at us. "Welcome to the Lotus Fine Art Gallery. How can I help you?"

"We're here to see Lotus," I smiled.

"Do you have an appointment?"

"No, but you can let her know Amos and Eugeena are here. We thought we'd come by and enjoy some of the beautiful artwork she's collected here."

"I will go find her. Please, take your time and enjoy."

We moved past the small lobby further into the gallery where rows of artwork beckoned us forward. All the pieces were so different, but all shared vibrant colors whether of people or places.

"Lotus certainly has an eye for talent," I murmured, pausing in front of a stunning oil painting of a woman wearing a large hat. The woman's hands stretched upward in praise. I bent down to read more about the artist.

"Wow! This was painted by Lotus. You know I should have recognized the style. It looks similar to that piece in Cinnamon's living room above the piano." I exclaimed, "It's so beautiful!"

"Thank you." I heard a voice behind us. We turned around to find Lotus standing in the doorway, her eyes wide with surprise. Today, she wore a simple black sleeveless dress that hugged her figure. Her gaze flicked between Amos and me before settling on me. "Eugeena... and Amos. What brings you two here?"

"Hello, Lotus. A few people have recommended we should come see your gallery. This is wonderful!"

Lotus offered a small smile as she drew closer to us. "I've poured my heart into this place. It means a lot to hear that."

She stopped a few feet from us and crossed her arms. I sensed our presence made her nervous, which made me more curious about her.

Lotus asked, "Would you like to join me in my office? We can talk more privately in there. I assume there's a purpose for this visit besides viewing my gallery."

She was very perceptive.

"Of course," Amos replied. He placed a gentle hand on the small of my back. "Lead the way, Lotus."

As we followed her through the gallery and into her office, I couldn't help but feel nervous myself. I'd seen Lotus's explosive temper with her mother. Amos and I had agreed to visit her, but we hadn't talked about what we were going to ask her.

Lotus had a large office in the back that had a stunning view of the surrounding buildings. Even though it was mid-morning, people bustled up and down the street.

I commented, "That's almost artwork outside your window there."

Lotus's smile widened. "I love it. I can peer out during the day and people watch, but the tinted glass shields me from prying eyes. Please, have a seat." She gestured to a pair of comfortable-looking white chairs across from her desk.

As I sat, I wondered if Lotus had the same interior designer as her mother or if the two women shared the same tastes. Lotus's office had light gray walls and white furnishing. But unlike her mother's plush carpeting, she had dark wood floors. She sat behind a very modern desk that looked like something out of a science fiction movie.

She waited until Amos and I had settled in the chairs before asking, "What can I do for you? I already know this has to be about my mother."

I held up a finger. "Actually, before we ask questions about your mother, I have one about Jared." I pulled out my phone. There was one photo in particular that had caught my eye last night. Though it hung in the section dedicated to Cinnamon, she wasn't in the photo. That struck me as odd, and I wondered if Olivia added the photo to the wall or someone else.

After I swiped to the photo, I turned my phone toward Lotus. "Is this Jared with his boy band?"

Lotus grimaced as if I'd hit her. "Yes. Where did you get that photo?"

"At the Blue Note Lounge. Olivia showed us the section that's dedicated to your mother."

She sighed. "Yeah, the Blue Note is a special place for Mom. I hadn't realized they put up a photo of the Lit Boys."

I frowned. "I used to be a social studies teacher and tried to keep up with the young people and their slang. Did you say 'Lit?'"

Lotus smiled. "From how my son explained it, Lit means to be excited. Those boys were definitely excited about singing." Her smile slipped from her face. "They practiced all the time at our house. I used to get mad at Jared that he had such an interest in music, but then I would hear him sing. I would be so proud of him."

Amos asked, "Can you tell us about the other three boys?"

Lotus leaned back in the seat and turned her face toward the window. "You may or may not have heard this, but one of them died last year. Lawrence Howard better known as Lars. He had been Jared's best friend since elementary school. When they got older, I pulled Jared out of public school and placed him in private school. Lars got into trouble, and I didn't want that influence to pass to Jared. Unfortunately, even though I kept them from attending the same school, they still hung out."

"I imagine when they started the boy band you preferred they practiced at your house." I offered.

"Absolutely. I tried to protect Jared. But he still got exposed to things I would rather he'd not." She swallowed and looked down at her desk. "He found Lars unconscious and tried to wake him up. That night broke my son. He's still not quite recovered, and he refuses to sing."

"I'm so sorry, Lotus."

It was such a shame how this young man lost his life so soon. That explained why Jared struggled with his own life without his friend. It was like his dream died too.

Amos inquired, "What happened to the other two boys?"

Lotus looked up, her eyes faraway. "Akeem and Brandon. They're brothers. They were both devastated, too. They moved from Nashville earlier this year. I heard they're out in California doing other things. Brandon always wanted to act more than sing anyway."

Amos asked, "So Jared wouldn't have reached out to them?"

Lotus grimaced. "I see where this is going. No, Jared was closer to Lars than the other two boys. The Lit Boys originally only had three members, but Lars insisted they invite Jared. Jared mentioned to me how awkward it was sometimes but they made it work."

Something occurred to me when Lotus mentioned Lars' last name. "You said Lars's last name was Howard. Out of curiosity, is he related to Tommy Howard, who plays the guitar in your mom's band?"

Lotus's face hardened and her eyes flashed. "Yes, Tommy is Lars's older brother. He had the nerve to accuse Jared of his brother's overdose. I wouldn't be surprised if Lars got the drugs that killed him from his own brother."

I glanced at Amos, who'd looked just as perplexed as me. "Well, Lotus, how did Tommy end up playing the guitar in your mom's band?"

Lotus narrowed her eyes. "That's a good question. I told my mother she would regret the day she ever hired him."

Chapter 16

I had some suspicions about Tommy when we met him at Niecy's salon two days ago. He seemed more interested in his money, and Niecy's warning for him to stay away from Jared seemed peculiar. Now I saw where a level of tension could exist between the two young men.

What I couldn't understand was why Cinnamon would let the man in her band? That had to be uncomfortable when Jared became her manager.

Then there was the business of Tommy being a mechanic. I didn't want to put too many of my thoughts in Lotus's ear, but I had to know more.

"Do you know who your mom takes her car to when it needs maintenance?"

Lotus raised her eyebrows at the switch in subject. "No. Why?"

Her question had me raising my eyebrows in response. "You know that someone messed with your mother's brakes? That's why she crashed."

Lotus's jaw dropped, and for a few uncomfortable seconds she stared at us. "I thought the detectives were questioning my mother about Jared."

Amos spoke up. "They were looking for Jared, but their first order of business was your mom's accident. Her car crash caused significant damage to that shop."

Lotus shook her head. "I know. Look, she never tells me anything. Jared knows more than me. I guess she doesn't trust me."

Before I could stop myself, I blurted. "Why is that?"

Lotus sighed heavily, her gaze drifting to the window and the bustling streets of Nashville beyond. "It wasn't always easy being the daughter of Cinnamon Waters. We've had our differences over the years, and sometimes I lashed out. But I've never wanted to harm her."

Amos looked at me, and then back at Lotus. "We're not here to accuse you, Lotus. We just want to find out who has it out for your mother."

"Thank you for not accusing me, but I needed to say that because when you asked about her car, I used it over the weekend. And Jared has her car most of the time. To be honest, she probably wouldn't have been driving herself yesterday day if Jared was around."

Amos frowned. "So, you also had access to her car?"

Lotus fidgeted in her seat. "That's right. But I'm not aware if the car went for any maintenance, at least not in the past few months."

That both Lotus and Jared were in and out of Cinnamon's car didn't ease my suspicions of them at all. Maybe I was barking up the wrong tree thinking Tommy could have been near the car. There was still that nagging question of what would have been his motive.

I had one more pressing question. "Lotus, did you talk to that reporter at the hospital? I believe his name is Ben Taylor. He mentioned on the news the other night that your mother has been unwell. That's pretty damaging."

The weight of the silence in the room bore down on us like a heavy fog. Lotus stared at her hands as if they were interesting pieces of art.

I...I did talk to a reporter," she admitted. "Last week, my mother and I had a nasty argument. Believe it or not, it had been a while. Anyway, she threw it in my face about how she helped me start the gallery as if that meant I owed her loyalty."

"Loyalty?" I asked.

Lotus's eyes teared up. "I met with Barry for lunch last Friday. I didn't tell my mother I was going to meet him, but I let her know afterwards. She was livid. Barry told me he thought my mother was unwell and that I should look into her health. I told Barry there was nothing wrong with my mother other than she had grown more into being a diva in her old age. I'd ran into that reporter before, and I felt like I needed to tell him something. I was hoping he would leave her alone. Ben Taylor has been digging around in my mom's life for years."

"Really?"

Lotus nodded. "A few months ago, he emailed me, claiming he was working on some unauthorized biography of her."

My eyebrows shot up in surprise at this revelation. "What? He can't do that."

Lotus grimaced. "He seemed to think he had the freedom to do it. I've seen other celebrities get unauthorized biographies. I'm just not sure why he thinks my mother is so interesting. I mean, sure, she has had a wonderful career, but she hasn't had a lot of drama around her."

Amos must have been thinking what I'd been thinking because he asked before me. "When you say the reporter reached out a few months ago, was that around the time your mother thought Barry had stolen from her?"

Lotus stared at him before responding. "You know what? It was around the same time. What does that mean?"

Amos shook his head. "I don't know. You know something has bothered me about this whole thing with Barry. Did he tell you, or do you know, what flagged Cinnamon to the stolen money?"

"Barry told me my mother noticed she had a substantial amount of money missing from her bank account. It was a little over $10,000. Whoever transferred funds out of her account did it in small increments over the past few months. My mother rarely pays attention to her bank statements. Believe it or not, she's not a big spender either. The most she has splurged on was when she bought that house a few years ago. And she really trusted Barry over the years to take care of things for her. In so many ways, he was more than a manager. "

I shook my head. "It's a shame they never got married."

"No, they had this Oprah and Stedman thing going on, but Barry would stray and date other women from time to time. My mother mainly stayed to herself. The only man I recall her being with was Barry. It's why I got to know him so well as a father figure. Even I knew he would never hurt my mother."

"So it sounds like Barry had some type of access to your mother's personal business, like where she put her money and her car." Amos asked.

"I know it sounds weird, but yes, she really trusted him. Until she didn't." Lotus looked at us both, squirming in her seat.

I took her discomfort to mean we'd taken up enough of her time. "We can leave. Thank you for talking to us."

"Wait." Lotus held up her hands. "I don't know if you know this, and I probably should have said something to the police. But really, the way they treated Jared like he was some drug dealer, I just wanted them to stay away from him."

"What is it?" I asked.

"When we were leaving from lunch last Friday, Barry told me he had hired a private detective to look into some things, but he didn't give me a name or any other details. He just said it was an old friend of his who owed him a favor."

That's what Cinnamon told us, too. Barry must have found out something, and that's why he was killed.

"I don't know if you know, but my mother planned Barry's funeral for tomorrow. She's going to have the repast at her house. I'm sure she would appreciate you both being there."

I nodded. "Lotus, do you think Jared will show up to say goodbye to Barry? I know you must be worried."

Lotus's eyes teared up. "I'm so worried about him. This isn't like him at all. I know he looks guilty, but he wouldn't hurt Barry or anyone."

"Something has him scared. Do you have any ideas?"

Lotus shook her head. "I don't know. I've gone over our conversation from the other night. I didn't want to say this in front of my mother because I know she's freaked out, but I think Jared saw something. From the way he was babbling the other night, he saw Barry get shot. Then, he said he hit the ground too. I don't know if he saw the shooter, but it scared him. The detectives have been at my home and here at the gallery. I know they don't believe me, but I honestly don't know where he would be all this time."

"We'll pray for his safety and that he will return soon."

We thanked Lotus and left. The sun shone bright in the sky and outside the art gallery, it beamed down. I glanced at my watch and realized it was lunchtime. I looked at Amos. "I know a funeral is not on your agenda for tomorrow."

Amos rubbed his forehead. "No, but there's no telling who will show up. I'm concerned about how Jared is staying away for so long. It makes me wonder if he's truly hiding or if something else happened to him."

"So we can plan to go to Cinnamon's house after the funeral. At least we can talk to more people."

As we ventured down the sidewalk away from the gallery, I asked Amos. "Do you think we can find out about this private detective? It sounds like this old friend of Barry's may have the information we need."

Amos agreed. "I thought about that after Lotus mentioned it. I can think of one person we can ask for help. From yesterday, it sounded like Jack Harris knew Barry the longest and the man sounds connected too. I'm going to hazard a guess he could be helpful. Or we can search for private detectives in the area, which I can tell you I definitely don't want to do."

That sounded like a solid plan to me. Jack Harris's words from yesterday had remained in the back of my mind.

I always felt like someone was manipulating her somehow.

Chapter 17

By Friday morning, my body had adjusted to the central time zone, and it wasn't as hard to get out of bed. As usual, Amos had jumped into the shower before me and headed downstairs to grab breakfast. Even though I was wide awake, I laid in bed staring at the patterned wallpaper, thinking about how far we'd strayed from our original plans for this trip. But despite the unexpected twists and turns, I couldn't deny that life was never dull with Amos by my side. With a bit more effort, I heaved myself up from the bed and headed into the shower.

When I opened the door to the steam-filled bathroom, I heard my phone buzzing from the nightstand. I hurried over, wrapping the bathrobe belt around my waist.

It was my aunt Cora.

My heart jumped in my chest when I realized she'd texted me and now was calling for the second time. I hoped this didn't mean something had gone wrong back home. If so, our trip would have to be cut short.

"Cora, hey, what's going on?" I sounded like I'd run a marathon.

"Hey, Eugeena, I hate to interrupt you on your honeymoon, but I noticed some posts on Facebook and it brought to mind a strange phone call I had the other day."

Cora was only a year older than me and was the youngest child on my dad's side. She shared a home with my oldest living aunt, Esther. Now a retired nurse and caregiver for her sister, Cora often checked up on me to see how I was doing. We both shared a love of Facebook. As boomers, we did little social media, but Facebook usually was a daily event.

I placed the phone on speaker so I could get dressed before Amos returned with breakfast. "A phone call? Who was it from?"

Cora's voice sounded even louder than usual, so I checked my volume. I told her a few weeks ago she might be losing her hearing, but she claimed it wasn't that bad. At least not bad enough to be walking around with hearing aids. Cora was a pretty woman and still dyed her hair. She hadn't taken to getting old very well. Probably because she was the youngest in her family and Aunt Esther was in her eighties. Cora would always be the baby and little sister despite being in her sixties.

Cora's voice hitched. "It was a man asking about Cinnamon Waters."

I stopped with my arm in mid-air. I'd been trying to push my arm through the shirt sleeve, but the mention of someone calling about Cinnamon Waters struck me cold. Sure, I'd seen the posts on Facebook last night. I felt a pang of sympathy for Cinnamon. It couldn't be easy having your private life splashed across the internet for all to see.

But why would someone be calling my Aunt Cora about Cinnamon?

Cora, who could not see me in the frozen state of getting dressed, continued talking, "Actually he was asking about Charlie."

I broke out of my stupor and finished putting on my shirt. I needed to be dressed to hear the rest of this. "What?" I sputtered. "He asked you about Charlie Waters?"

"Yeah. He said something about writing a biography about Cinnamon Waters. He wanted to interview people who knew her during her time in Charleston. He was interested in finding out how her brother died. I hadn't heard anyone mention Charlie Waters in over forty years. It was the strangest call."

I immediately knew who'd called Cora. I couldn't believe that reporter had somehow gotten ahold of my aunt's phone number. Sure, Cora was in the phone book and she never married, so her name had not changed over the years. But Ben Taylor was digging too hard for his unauthorized biography on Cinnamon.

"So what did you say to him?" I asked.

"I told him there was nothing I could tell him. Everything he wanted to know about Charlie Waters was on public record. Then I hung up on him. Anyway, you remember the papers and news covered his death pretty well."

"You're right. They did." My mother had passed by then, and Daddy was the sole parent in the house. "I remember Daddy wouldn't let me watch the news, but I saw the write up in his newspaper."

"That was my older brother. He always was protecting his only girl."

I had to smile at that.

Cora huffed. "You know I hadn't seen Cinnamon Waters in years. I remember she came down for Ralph's funeral, but I didn't have a chance to talk to her. She was in and out, but I know you appreciated seeing her. You both were so close back then."

I didn't want anyone back home knowing what Amos and I had been up to all week. I could hear the fussing now, but I couldn't keep this from Cora. "You will not believe this, but Amos treated me to see Cinnamon onstage at the Blue Note Lounge on Monday."

Cora screeched. "What? Oh, no. You were both there during the shooting?"

"It wasn't a mass shooting. Barry Jenkins was the target. He had been more than a manager to Cinnamon over the years, so you can imagine she took it pretty hard."

I figured that was good enough to tell Cora for now. She didn't need to know about the threats Cinnamon had received or she would have me and Amos on the next flight out of Nashville.

"We're going to see her in a few hours to support her during the funeral."

Cora sucked in a breath. "Eugeena, I know you are a good friend, but please don't tell me you and Amos are going to a funeral during your honeymoon. What does Amos have to say about this? Have you and Amos even enjoyed yourselves? I mean, how is it you leave Charleston and still get into some of the same mess?"

During Cora's rant, which could have been a lot worse, Amos strode in with breakfast. He eyed my phone on the table. By the time it registered to him it was Cora, he was stifling laughter. Amos found it particularly funny whenever one of my aunts, whether Cora or Esther, told me a thing or two about myself.

That's probably because they were the only two people who really could set me straight. Probably had to do with the fact they were my daddy's sisters. My daddy was an incredibly strict man. The second reason was they were the only two aunts I had who lived close to me. I never really knew my mother's people because Mama moved down south from New York. There was a whole slew of relatives I had no clue about.

I interrupted Cora's fussing. "You're not telling me something that I hadn't thought about. But you know if someone's in trouble that I'm gonna help." I glanced over at Amos, who'd set the breakfast out on the table. "Amos is here with our breakfast. He's been a real trooper. "

Amos chuckled. "Don't worry, Cora. We've been having the time of our lives."

Cora sighed deeply on the phone. "That's good to hear from you. Don't let nothing else mess up this trip. It took you all too long to take it."

I pulled a seat out at the table. My stomach grumbled as the smell of bacon assaulted my senses. "I agree. Anyway, we only have a limited time in Nashville now. We check out of the hotel on Sunday morning, and Amos has planned some time for us down in Memphis."

"Okay, well, let me let y'all get to eating. Eugeena, you can wait to do this when you get back, but I bet that man reached out to you. Probably left a message on your house landline."

I said goodbye and ended the call.

Amos stared at me. "What man?"

"Oh, I need to tell you why Cora called."

I recapped Ben Taylor calling Cora to ask about Charlie and explained to Amos. "Charlie was in the same class as Cora. We all lived in the same area."

Amos chewed, his forehead crinkled in concentration. "So, he's going through your high school yearbook to find people."

"Sounds about right. Cora would be the easiest one to locate since she never married. I imagine he probably called me too, but he doesn't know we're here in Nashville."

Amos picked up his phone and started dialing.

I frowned. "What are you doing?"

"I want to know if he called. I'm going to retrieve our messages."

And Cora wanted to accuse me of being the one getting into things. When Amos Jones wanted to know something, he had no problem with investigating right on the spot.

We both waited as he listened to our messages. He commented, "Out of the entire week, there were only three messages. Two were from politicians wanting our donations. This is the other." He placed his phone down on the table, turning on the speakerphone.

"Hello, this is Ben Taylor. I'm working on a biography of Cinnamon Waters. I would love to talk to you about your friendship with her. I understand you both were good friends many years ago. When you get this message, if you could, please call me."

Amos looked at me as the man rattled off his phone number. Then stated it again.

It's a good thing I had finished my breakfast because the sound of the man's voice made me ill. "You're not expecting me to call him back. I definitely don't want to talk to him."

"I don't think we should talk to him. Not yet."

I raised an eyebrow. "What do you mean, not yet?"

Amos nodded. "There are going to be a lot of eyes on Barry's funeral in a few hours. I'm not a betting man, but if Mr. Taylor was so bold to show up at Cinnamon's hospital room, what would keep him from this funeral?"

I cringed, hoping I wouldn't have to run into Ben Taylor today.

He'd already gotten on my last nerve and I hadn't met him yet.

Chapter 18

Amos and I watched the mourners file into the mega-church from a pew in the back. The air was heavy with sadness and thick with the scent of lilies. Either Barry Jenkins had been a popular man with many wanting to give a proper farewell or because of the views from certain social media outlets, some came for fireworks.

Really not too different from most funerals.

I whirled my head back and forth, looking for one person in particular.

Amos predicted that Ben Taylor would show up like other curious observers. The only difference was the reporter would come with the sole purpose of digging up dirt on people. I still couldn't believe he had the nerve to reach out to my Aunt Cora and had left messages on my phone back home. I just hoped everything went smoothly at the funeral today because there was no doubt Ben Taylor would be in front of a camera with his big tooth smile and fancy toupee.

At that very moment, the man entered the church, looking around like a snake searching for its prey.

"Speak of the devil," I muttered under my breath.

"Told you," Amos chuckled. "That man is way too interested in Cinnamon's life to not show up at the funeral of her manager."

"And lover boy," I added. "They sure had a complicated relationship. Still, that's not enough for a whole biography."

The choir entered the loft as clergy climbed the steps to the pulpit. It was time. I craned my neck around a woman who'd sat in front of me with one of those big church hats. The rings around the hat looked like she had the planet of Saturn on top of her head.

Cinnamon sat up front. Next to her was Lotus. Both women were dressed in black. Cinnamon wore a simple hat with a black netted veil, while Lotus's hair was swept up into a bun. They both stared at the casket in front of them, which was closed at the moment.

Niecy and Tommy sat on the row behind them along with other members of the band.

Jared remained missing. I really didn't know what to think about the situation. The young man hadn't shown up at the hospital for his grandmother, hadn't been in touch with his mother, and now a man that had been a part of his entire life was being eulogized. Jared not showing his face felt suspicious. Either he was responsible for the man's death or something serious had happened to him. I hoped the latter wasn't the case. He probably single-handedly kept what little relationship Cinnamon had with Lotus going.

In my peripheral, I saw where Detective Davis and Detective Harris sat. Of course, they would attend the funeral too. I was sure their focus was on bringing the elusive young man into custody.

The choir sang familiar hymns, and the pastor preached way too long, but nothing out of the ordinary occurred. That was until the funeral director directed his staff to open the casket. We were too far away to see Barry Jenkins in his final resting place, but the sight set off a wave of emotion as people strained to see.

A low wail rose near the front. Then it turned high pitch, sending ushers rushing from each side of the church. My heart hurt as I realized the source of the tragic cries was coming from my dear friend.

Oh, Cinnamon.

At least three ushers surrounded her, one with a box of tissues, another had squeezed in between Cinnamon and Lotus, rubbing Cinnamon's back. One stood in front as if to block anyone from viewing Cinnamon in her grief.

The crowd would not allow us to get near Cinnamon, so we tumbled outside. Most of the week had been bright and sunny. But today, clouds gathered above us. As people continued to disperse out of the church, I caught sight of Ben Taylor standing with his phone in hand.

I wondered what he was typing. I glanced over at Amos, who followed my head nod toward the reporter.

"Let's go," he said.

We swerved around bodies standing in the way until we reached the reporter. "Mr. Taylor, I believe?" I said, extending my hand. "Eugeena Patterson-Jones. This is my husband, Amos Jones. You left a message on our home phone."

Ben Taylor's eyebrows shot up, making his face appear almost comical. "Mrs. Patterson! What a... pleasure to finally meet you," he stammered. "I didn't expect to see you here, in Nashville of all places."

"I'm sure you didn't," I replied. My voice sounded way more polite than I felt.

Ben's eyes gleamed with excitement, no doubt seeing a golden opportunity to pry information from me. "I know this isn't the best time, but I would love to talk to you. I'm assuming you are in town to support your friend Ms. Waters."

"Mr. Taylor," I said, placing my hands on my hips and trying to remain composed, "I'm not here to speak to you about Cinnamon or her personal life." I looked back at Amos, and then turned to Ben Taylor, narrowing my eyes. "Actually, we have a question for you."

He looked taken aback. Looking from me to Amos, I thought the man would take off running. But a sly smile spread across his thin lips making me not like him even more.

"Please, ask away."

"Out of all the music celebrities in Nashville, why are you writing about Cinnamon Waters? Not that I don't think my friend has not had an illustrious career, but why do you think you could sell books about her life? An unauthorized biography at that." I questioned.

"You know, Mrs. Patterson," he began, "the little stories of people like Cinnamon can be bestsellers too. It's not always about the glitz and glamour of the big stars. Sometimes it's the personal tragedies that really grip readers."

"Tragedies?" I asked. I could feel Amos stiffen beside me.

"Indeed," Ben continued, oblivious, or not caring that Amos and I had to be looking at him like he'd lost his mind. "Cinnamon had quite a past, you know. Her older brother was murdered when she was just a teenager. She's never spoken about it to anyone. Can you imagine the impact that must have had on her?"

My mouth dropped open. Cinnamon had been devastated by her brother's death. The idea of someone exploiting that pain for profit sickened me. But there was something else in Ben's words, something I couldn't quite put my finger on at first. And then it hit me.

"Are you insinuating that Cinnamon had something to do with her brother's death?" I demanded. "I grew up with the family. What happened is on record."

"Mrs. Patterson," he barreled forward, "then you know the family left town shortly after Charlie Waters was killed."

Was he really trying to turn Charlie's death into a story he could exploit? I could barely contain my frustration with this man, but I took a deep breath. "Do you have children, Mr. Taylor?" I held up my hand. "Don't answer that. If your child or a member of your family was brutally murdered, would you want to stay in the same town? Or would you pack up your family and leave to find some semblance of peace?"

He hesitated for a moment before replying. "Of course I see the circumstances would have been difficult. But there are more unexplained deaths in Cinnamon's past than just her brother."

"Are you implying that Cinnamon is somehow responsible for these so-called 'unexplained deaths?'"

Ben shrugged nonchalantly. "I'm not making any accusations, but the public has a right to know about all aspects of their favorite singer's life, don't they?"

"Her private life is no one's business!"

Amos held my elbow, and I looked at him, then around us. Most people had left the parking lot to head to the cemetery, but a few stragglers looked curiously at us.

I tried to calm my nerves, which was hard to do because Mr. Taylor had my stomach in knots.

Amos asked, "Who's your source, Mr. Taylor? If you're so sure of your facts, then surely you have no qualms sharing their identity with me."

Ben leaned back, crossing his arms over his chest. "I never give up a source, Mr. Jones. But I can assure you, my information is legitimate. My source is close enough to Cinnamon to know the truth."

My heart raced at the thought of someone close to Cinnamon. Who would betray her like this? And why would they make accusations like that to a reporter?

My mind shot to Lotus. When we talked to her yesterday at her gallery, she mentioned she told the reporter her mother had been unwell. What else did Lotus say that she didn't confess to?

Ben gave us a smug smile. "Maybe there's more to her than you think. "

"Or maybe," I retorted, "you've just found someone who wants to cash in on Cinnamon's fame by feeding you lies. Did you ever consider that?"

"Trust me," he replied confidently. "The information I received is solid."

"Solid?" I scoffed. "You ought to be ashamed of yourself, Mr. Taylor."

He shrugged. "I'm just doing my job. It was good talking to you."

We watched the reporter saunter off as though he'd just dropped a bomb. I wasn't sure if he did or not, but the whole conversation left me disturbed.

"Are you alright, Eugeena?" Amos's gentle voice penetrated my thoughts.

"I'm not sure," I sighed. "What do you think he was talking about? He said unexplained deaths. Bringing up Charlie made no sense. I could see him referring to Barry's death, but he tried to say there were other people who died."

Amos threw his arm around my shoulder. "I'm sure he's just digging for a story. I hate to say it, but the man is old and past his prime. To compete in today's media market, he probably has to find a sensational story that will get him fifteen minutes in the spotlight."

"Mmmm, well, I hope the spotlight turns on him."

But we were back to the theories that had swirled around all week.

Cinnamon's enemy was very close.

Too close.

Chapter 19

The air was heavy with sorrow as Amos and I entered Cinnamon's house. It still seemed strange to have the repast in her home, but then Cinnamon had planned the funeral. I guessed she wanted to open her home to people who knew Barry best.

Several familiar faces greeted us, including Olivia Harris. Her eyes were red-rimmed and puffy from tears. I knew it took a lot for her to be in Cinnamon's home. I hoped the two women could make up and reconcile their friendship.

I spotted Niecy and Tommy standing near the fireplace, both looking rather uncomfortable among the crowd of mourners. Niecy's face brightened when she caught sight of us. She quickly made her way over with Tommy trailing behind. Tommy glanced around as if searching for a chance to escape.

"Ms. Eugeena and Mr. Amos," Niecy said. "I'm so glad you could make it. Cinnamon will really appreciate your support."

"Of course, dear. We wouldn't miss it for the world," I replied. Amos nodded in agreement, his eyes searching the room. Old habits die hard, I suppose. He touched my arm and told me he was going to get us something to drink. But I knew Amos was going to work the room. I knew he would mingle instead of coming back right away. That was the whole reason we came. Sure, we were there to support Cinnamon. But someone wanted to harm her and we needed to find out who.

I watched Amos cross the room. He stopped to talk with Jack Harris. Amos had called him last night. Maybe the man would come through and help us find this private detective Barry supposedly hired.

Someone swore beside me, and I realized Tommy had been grumbling out loud. I looked over my glasses at him. "Is everything alright, Tommy?" I asked. Maybe he didn't like funerals or death. Only yesterday we'd learned that Tommy had tragedies in his own family. Losing a younger brother had to hit hard.

Tommy avoided eye contact with me. "This whole situation is messed up. And no one has seen Jared yet. Everybody pretends like he's so good."

Niecy whirled on him. "This is not the time or place for this again."

Tommy snarled, "Yeah, whatever! Did you hear how hard Cinny cried? Was she for real? Barry probably flipped over in that coffin."

Niecy glared at him. "Nobody asked for your opinion or for you to come."

Tommy looked ready to smack Niecy but grunted instead. "I'm out of here." He walked off like the whole thing disgusted him.

Having to witness these two at each other, I was happy he left. But Tommy had brought up the elephant in the room. Jared wasn't at the funeral. It didn't make sense because no matter how things went down with Barry, surely he would pay his respects to the man. And even more importantly, why would he have his mother and grandmother worried about him?

From across the room, I noticed Lotus standing next to a man who appeared to be her age. But I didn't see any signs of Cinnamon.

"Where's Cinnamon?" I asked Niecy.

She peered around. "I don't know. She was in the kitchen. That's her spot. I heard she was in there all night baking cakes and pies, although her arm was in that sling. I guess Lotus helped."

I could relate to the kitchen being a comfort zone. "That's nice that Lotus could spend some time with her mother." I wondered if our talk with Lotus at her gallery yesterday softened her feelings toward her mother at all. They both needed each other. I prayed nothing had happened to Jared. If so, they would need each other even more.

Niecy furrowed her brow. "I guess. We'll see how long it lasts. Sometimes Lotus is even nice to me if it benefits her."

"You two really don't get along."

Niecy shrugged. "I guess she never got over Cinnamon taking me into her home."

I frowned. "But Lotus would have been out of the house back then. She would have been raising Jared, right?"

Niecy nodded. "Yep. Jared spent a lot of time with Cinnamon too, so we practically grew up together. I don't know what it was. Maybe Lotus wanted Cinnamon to pour all her attention into Jared. In my opinion, Cinnamon did that. Not that I ever wanted for anything, but Jared is her favorite."

"I see." Or didn't see. I was sure there was more to why Lotus despised Niecy, but now wasn't the time. "I'm concerned about Jared. You never found him." I leveled my gaze at her. My glasses had slid down to the tip of my nose the same way when I was berating a student. "I could understand with you two being so close that you would respect his wishes for not being found."

Niecy flicked her eyes away from me and stepped back slightly.

Does she know where he is?

If she did, she wasn't about to reveal his whereabouts to me. She shook her head and stuttered. "I've been looking for him, too. I've called and texted. I can't find him anywhere. I promise I don't know where he is. I'm worried like everyone else."

"I believe you, Niecy. And I have to ask, I recently learned that Jared's friend, Lars was Tommy's brother. Is that why Tommy seems so mad at Jared?"

Niecy fidgeted beside me. "Tommy knows better, but he felt like Jared could have saved his brother. But no one could have saved Lars from himself. I just hope Jared hasn't done something."

"Like what?" I asked.

Did Niecy also think Jared shot Barry?

She turned and looked at me, her eyes fierce with concern. "Like hurt himself. Jared should be here. He loved Barry like a father. I never imagined he wouldn't be here."

That's something that had stirred in my mind, but I hoped the young man hadn't hurt himself. Where was he that no one could find him?

At that moment, Cinnamon appeared, trying to balance what appeared to be a pie plate with one hand. A tall, thin man with long fingers walked up to Cinnamon and grabbed the plate from her. She looked startled to see the man as he placed the pie on the table.

The man turned toward her and stuffed his hands into his pants pockets as he spoke to Cinnamon. She awkwardly held his gaze by lifting her eyes to meet his.

"Who's that?" I whispered to Niecy, nodding toward the man. She squinted for a moment before recognition dawned on her face.

"That's Nate Parker," she replied. "Her former guitar player. Tommy replaced him."

My curiosity piqued, I watched as Nate tried to speak to Cinnamon. She rebuffed him, her eyes filled with distress and emotional turmoil. It was clear she didn't want to entertain any conversation with him, and within moments, she turned and walked away, leaving Nate standing there, looking lost and confused.

I observed Nate's crestfallen expression.

Niecy shook her head. "I don't know why Nate or Olivia bothered to come to Cinnamon's house. She's not going to talk to either of them."

"Didn't you tell me that Nate was in love with Olivia?"

Niecy hesitated for a moment before answering, "Yeah, they were involved for a while too. But it ended badly, like most of his relationships. Jack has been better for her."

I scanned the room and saw Amos was no longer talking to Jack. I watched as Olivia walked up to her husband, a stricken look on her face. Most people would have seen Cinnamon walk away from Nate. That probably didn't make Olivia comfortable. This was like watching a soap opera play out, which I had to admit was a common theme at most funerals I had attended over the years. A funeral could bring out either the best or worst in people.

Many people had left since Amos and I arrived, only a few remained. I decided to introduce myself to Nate Parker before he took off. In theory, I was sure this wasn't a good idea with Cinnamon showing her irritation earlier.

"Excuse me, Mr. Parker?" I said softly, not wanting to startle him. He turned to face me, a flicker of surprise registering in his eyes. Then his expression turned into one of polite interest.

"Please," he said, extending a hand for me to shake, "call me Nate."

"Alright, Nate." I stretched out my right hand to flash my wedding ring just in case Nate had any ideas. "I'm Eugeena Patterson-Jones, a friend of Cinnamon."

"Ah, yes," he nodded, his grip firm yet warm. "She mentioned your name a few times. It's a pleasure to finally meet you, although I wish it were under better circumstances."

I studied Nate more closely. There was something about him—a quiet sadness. "Were you and Barry close friends?"

He grinned. "Indeed, I've known Barry a long time. I truly hope he's at peace. He didn't always treat Cinny the best, but he loved and cared for her."

"I understand Cinnamon hasn't seemed like herself for quite some time now. About a year, at least."

"Is that so?" Nate's eyes darted around the room, his shoulders tense as he fidgeted with the cuff of his sleeve. I could tell he was uncomfortable, but when else would I have a chance to talk to him?

He swallowed hard and shifted his weight from one foot to the other, seemingly unable to stand still. "Well, you know how it is in this business. The road can be tough on all of us, especially as we get older."

"True enough," I agreed. "But it seems like more than just age or exhaustion. She doesn't trust anyone anymore. Have you noticed anything like that?" I searched Nate's face, not sure what I was looking for. Maybe I wanted to see him angry.

Nate hesitated, his eyes flicking toward the door as if he were contemplating leaving instead. But then he sighed and ran a hand over his salt-and-pepper low cut fade.

"Yeah," he admitted. "I've noticed it too. Something's changed in her, and it's been going on for a while now. But I don't know what it is. I wish I did."

That wasn't what I wanted to hear, and I knew the disappointment had spread across my face. "We chatted with Olivia earlier this week," I mentioned. "She's just as concerned about Cinnamon as we are."

Nate commented, "I'm glad you guys talked to her. She's known Cinnamon even longer than I have, and I know how much their blow up hurt her."

I nodded. "She told me and my husband about how Cinnamon seemed to get paranoid, thinking Olivia was sabotaging her career."

Nate's eyes flashed. "Cinny was off-base. And it made little sense since Olivia did her own thing for years, anyway. It didn't bother Cinny since she'd slowed down on gigs over the years. It was time for Olivia to shine some."

The man was certainly passionate about Olivia. I wondered if he still held a torch for her. Like she was the one that got away.

"What about you? I saw pictures of the band back in the day on the Blue Note Lounge wall. You were with the band a long time too."

"Almost twenty years. Cinny changed overnight. I talked to Olivia, asked if maybe something was going on with her health-wise. We're all in our sixties now and we've been doing this music thing for a long time."

I nodded, understanding the toll that years in the spotlight could take on a person. "Do you remember any specific incident that might have triggered this change?"

"Nothing comes to mind," Nate replied, his brow furrowed as he tried to recall. "It's more like she just started pulling away from everyone, bit by bit."

"Did anything happen between you two that upset her?" I ventured, hoping to get a better sense of why Cinnamon lost her longtime guitar player.

"Actually, it started with a song choice," Nate continued, his brow furrowed. "Cinnamon had an unusual outburst over it.

It wasn't like her at all. You know she can sing anything – blues, jazz, R&B, even country. So, it just didn't add up."

A song!

I pressed. "Was it a song that meant something to her personally, or did she just not like it?"

Nate shook his head slowly. "I don't think so. It wasn't a song she'd ever mentioned as being special to her. She just... She was adamant that we shouldn't perform it. And it was so unlike her to get upset like that."

As Nate spoke, I couldn't help but feel there must be something more to the story. Amos kept telling me there was something Cinnamon had been holding back. Did this song have anything to do with whatever other secret Cinnamon was hiding? The person threatening her had been very specific that Cinnamon had done something.

"What song was it, Nate?" I asked, trying to keep my voice steady despite the urgency bubbling within me. "Maybe if we can figure out why it upset her so much, we'll be one step closer to understanding what's going on."

Nate hesitated for a moment, but just as he opened his mouth to speak, an ear-piercing scream rang through the house, causing the entire room to silence.

"Cinnamon!" I gasped, recognizing her voice instantly. There was no mistaking the raw terror that laced her cries, and I felt the blood drain from my face. Whatever was happening, I knew it was serious.

I saw Amos heading toward the stairs, so I followed close behind, my heart pounding in my chest as I willed my aging limbs to move faster.

Please, Lord, I prayed silently as we climbed the stairs. My mind was racing. *Protect Cinnamon from any further harm.*

Chapter 20

Cinnamon's house was unfamiliar to us, but I followed Amos up the stairs as if we'd been to her home a hundred times. Though her home had been built in recent years, the steps creaked and I couldn't help but feel like we were moving toward danger. The screaming had stopped, and an eerie silence replaced it, making the situation even more unnerving.

"Stay close, Eugeena," Amos said.

I could hear the contained panic in his voice. "I'm right behind you, Amos." My heart pounded in my chest.

We finally reached the top of the stairs. I looked left and saw a light coming from a room. Amos and I headed in that direction and soon stood in front of a large bedroom. Cinnamon had spared no expense with her bedroom. Plush white carpet led into an extravagant bedroom adorned with elegant furniture and soft pink walls.

No doubt the master bedroom.

Just inside the doorway, Lotus stood frozen, her hand covering her mouth, her eyes wide with shock.

"Lotus, what happened?" I asked as I rushed toward her.

"Mom... she..." Lotus stuttered, unable to form complete sentences. My mind raced with possibilities, each one worse than the last.

"Is she alright?" I felt bad about walking on Cinnamon's pretty white carpet, but she sounded like she could be hurt.

We approached an open door, which appeared to lead into the master bathroom. I strained to hear anything beyond the eerie silence other than my heart pounding in my chest and practically in my ears.

Suddenly, Cinnamon stumbled out, her eyes wide with fear.

"Lord have mercy!" Amos exclaimed, rushing forward to catch her as she nearly collapsed. I hurried over too, taking her arm and guiding her toward the king-size bed draped in luxurious fabrics.

Cinnamon mumbled, her voice trembling as she fought back tears. "They're...in my house."

"Good Lord! Who?"

"Please...you have to believe me," she pleaded. In her eyes, I saw not only fear but also a desperate need for understanding.

"Of course we believe you," Amos reassured her. "You're not alone, Cinnamon. We're here for you. Tell us who is bothering you."

Tears rolled down her cheek as she repeated, her voice growing weaker. "They're here, in my house... and they won't stop until..."

"Until what?" I prodded.

"Until they destroy me," Cinnamon finished, her voice barely a whisper. The weight of her words hung heavy in the air.

Cinnamon's hands shook as she pointed toward the bathroom. "Look at what they put on my mirror!"

I hesitated for only a moment before hurrying into the master bathroom. The scent of Cinnamon's expensive perfume I'd grown familiar with the past few days lingered in the air. The vanity lights reflected off the polished marble floor casting a dim glow.

Then I saw it.

"Lord have mercy," I whispered under my breath as I read the chilling message scrawled across the mirror in bold strokes of red lipstick.

'I KNOW WHAT YOU DID'

The words seemed to loom larger than life, overshadowing the otherwise pristine bathroom. I felt my stomach twist into knots as a cold sliver of dread worked its way up my spine. This was something you saw in a Lifetime movie, not in real life.

"Call the police, Amos," my voice shook. "They need to see this."

"Right away, Eugeena," Amos's voice sounded grave. I spun around to find he'd followed me into the bathroom to see the message too. He held the phone up to his ear and beckoned me out of the bathroom.

He didn't have to ask me twice. I moved out of there as if someone or something had been chasing me. As I returned to Cinnamon's side, I couldn't help but think Cinnamon was right. Whoever wanted to harm her had been in her house and had the audacity to taunt her with a message in her own master bathroom.

"Did you see it, Eugeena?" Cinnamon's voice trembling with fear. "It's just like the other threats."

"Yes, I saw it," I replied, forcing myself to sound calm. "Amos is calling the police."

"Thank you, Eugeena," Cinnamon whispered. "I know this was not in you and Amos's plans when you came here, but I feel that God sent you both here."

"Lotus!" Amos called out, his voice firm and authoritative as he strode toward the young woman. "I just called the police. I know some people have left, but is there a list of who all came to the house?"

Lotus nodded, her gaze flicking to the bathroom before she turned away. "We had a guest book at the door, but I'm not sure who all signed it. Most of the people who came were band members and people who worked with my mom and Barry over the years."

I walked over to the door where Amos stood talking to Lotus. "Can you get the guest book, Lotus? The police will take it."

Amos raised an eyebrow at me.

"Or maybe just take pictures of the pages. I'm curious to know who was here." My mind also raced. I didn't need to walk back into that bathroom to see the message 'I KNOW WHAT YOU DID' — those words seemed to burn into my brain. I thought back to the other threats Cinnamon received.

We all had skeletons in our closets.

But what had Cinnamon done?

Lotus returned upstairs with the guest book. Amos wanted her to put it back so he snapped photos quickly using his phone.

Beside me, Cinnamon's voice quivered. "I think... I think I know who's doing this."

I turned, startled that she made an accusation. "Who?"

But then I noticed how she eyed her daughter.

"Sweetie," I said softly. "I know you're scared but accusing your own daughter... That's a heavy burden to lay on anyone, especially someone you love."

Cinnamon looked at me with tear-streaked eyes. "I saw her, Eugeena. I saw Lotus come out of my room just before I found that message on the mirror."

I took a deep breath, fighting against the knot in my stomach. "Did you see her actually write the message?" I asked gently.

"No, but who else could it be?" Cinnamon's voice trembled.

"Maybe she was in there for some other reason," I offered, trying to give her an alternate explanation.

Cinnamon shook her head, unconvinced. "I don't know, Eugeena. It just feels like everything is falling apart around me, and I don't know who to trust anymore."

Lotus noticed her mother staring at her, frowned and stepped forward. "What's wrong?"

Cinnamon wouldn't look at her daughter.

Lotus's eyes flashed with hurt and anger. "I know you don't think I did this. Mom, I only went into your room to use the bathroom because the ones downstairs were occupied. I didn't write anything on the mirror. I tried to warn you about it before you stepped in the bathroom."

"Lotus," Cinnamon sobbed, "I'm sorry for not being there for you when you needed me. But why... why would you do this to me?"

My heart ached for both of them. Cinnamon's fear was palpable, and her accusations clearly hurt Lotus.

Amos and I exchanged glances. I knew his eyes mirrored the despair in mine and the deep desire to escape all of this drama.

"Cinnamon," I said gently, placing a hand on her arm. "Maybe you should take a moment to think about what you're saying."

Lotus stood tall, defiant even in her pain. "Did you see me with lipstick, Mama?"

Cinnamon shook her head. "I just don't know who else could do this. You have hated me your whole life."

Lotus threw her hands in the air. "Now you're just being overly dramatic. Mom, I know things have been difficult." Her eyes filled with tears. "But I would never do anything to hurt you like that. I love you, even if we don't always see eye to eye. I see now that things will never change between us."

"Lotus—" I tried to intervene, but she held up her hand, silencing me.

"You can't help her. Something is wrong, and it's not with me." Lotus stepped closer to Cinnamon. "I don't know what's wrong with you, but you've pushed everyone away and it doesn't make sense."

She spun around and jabbed her finger toward me. "Watch yourself before she pushes you away, too," Lotus warned me. With that, she stormed out of the room.

That's when I noticed the same detectives from the hospital standing outside the bedroom. Their stern faces made my stomach knot up with anxiety.

What all did they hear? Did they hear Cinnamon accusing her daughter?

What a mess!

Chapter 21

The detectives made everyone leave the bedroom so they could address the situation. After making the trek downstairs, Amos and I made a beeline over to the food table. I ate when my nerves were bad, and this whole ordeal had worked up an appetite. I grabbed a plate and stared at the arrangement of sandwiches, veggies and ranch dressing. Amos and I looked at each other, his face mirroring my dismay.

It was already unusual that Cinnamon had coordinated the funeral arrangements for Barry. But this spread of food wasn't what I expected. But then again, I'd been to too many funerals during my lifetime, so maybe my expectations were too high. I hadn't been to a repast that didn't offer a plate of fried chicken, string beans, macaroni and cheese, a Hawaiian roll and a hunk of pound cake.

But this entire honeymoon trip hadn't been normal.

Niecy came up behind us. "With Cinnamon being in the hospital, some things got skipped. She has more baked goods in the kitchen. Follow me."

A few minutes later, Amos and I huddled in the kitchen at the breakfast nook eating pound cake and a slice of apple cobbler. The kitchen felt cozy.It was homier than the rest of the house. Cinnamon's personality could be felt from the hanging pots to the row of herbs in the windowsills.

Niecy offered us sweet tea from a pitcher. Since we had overloaded our sweet tooth, I asked for water.

She placed bottled water on the breakfast nook table and said, "I take it something happened upstairs. I saw Lotus up there, so I stayed down here. But everyone could hear them yelling."

The argument between Cinnamon and Lotus still disturbed me. "Yes. It seems someone has been threatening Cinnamon."

Niecy's eyes opened wide, and she stood with her mouth open for several seconds. "What? Why would someone threaten Cinnamon? Barry gets shot. Jared is missing. This is getting too scary!"

"I agree." I scraped the last remnants of the pound cake and sat the plate down. It was fantastic and though it wasn't a full meal, it was better than the rabbit food.

I looked at Niecy. "Did you see any guests go upstairs?"

She shook her head. "Not guests. Just Lotus, and then Cinnamon."

I glanced at Amos. Well, Niecy confirmed what Cinnamon said. I still believed Lotus. What reason would she have to taunt her mother?

Amos placed his plate in the sink. "Let's get back out there and see who's still here."

A quick scan of the living room showed Nate was still here. Tommy had stormed off earlier. Jack and Olivia had also left. I could tell Olivia was ready to go the last time I saw her.

Cinnamon sat on the couch, while Lotus stood behind, her eyes boring into the back of her mother's head. If looks could kill, I was super scared for Cinnamon. Someone wanted to take Cinnamon out of this world, and in her mind, she'd concluded it could be her daughter.

And what if it was Lotus?

Lotus huffed and turned away from her mother as though she could no longer stand the sight of her. Cinnamon seemed oblivious to her daughter's angst and stared at nothing in particular in front of her. I felt for my friend, but I was torn between wanting to comfort her or grabbing Amos and making a dash for the door.

Unfortunately, a deputy stood near the front door. No one else was leaving soon. I wondered if the real culprit had gotten away or if they remained inside the house waiting to be questioned.

I turned to Amos and tried to keep my voice low, "What do you think? Could Lotus be involved in any of this?"

He hesitated for a moment. "I don't want to believe she is, but... What if mother and son are working together? What if they're trying to get Cinnamon's money? It's like she's slowly been losing it, and they could be using that to their advantage."

I knew Amos had his theories and he could be objective, but I couldn't. Or, I just didn't want to believe that Cinnamon's own family members would do her harm.

At that moment, the detectives arrived downstairs and pulled Cinnamon aside to talk to her. The air hung thick with tension as they exited the room and entered through two French doors. From what I could see before the doors shut, it was the dining room.

Amos grabbed his phone from his pocket and peered down. He looked at me. "It's Jack."

I nodded, watching as Amos answered the call.

"Did you? Okay? In the morning? Sure thing. We will be there."

Amos said goodbye and slipped the phone back into his pocket.

From listening to the one-sided conversation, I hoped it was good news for a change. "Well, what did he say? I saw you talking to him earlier. I guess he and Olivia left before all the commotion."

Amos nodded. "Yeah, they didn't stay long. Olivia really didn't want to come. He told me earlier that he thought he knew who Barry could have hired to do the investigation."

"That's good. Maybe we can finally get some answers."

I took a deep breath to steady my nerves. We only had one full day left in Nashville, and I hated to admit it, but I was ready to leave all of this behind. What should have been our romantic getaway had turned into pure chaos.

I woke up earlier on Saturday than I had the entire week. Amos hadn't stirred yet, and he always woke up before me. Last night, the police took our statements quickly, and we left. They ordered Cinnamon to spend the night elsewhere, and she opted for a hotel. I wondered what would happen to my friend if the police didn't find the culprit who invaded not only her home, but her life. As I tried to drift off to sleep, fear seized my mind.

With our trip coming to an end here in Nashville, we might not know what would happen with Cinnamon.

We had to be missing something. Maybe the culprit was the MIA Jared or his bitter mother, Lotus. What if they had been working together? What if it was someone else we hadn't considered?

The one disturbing factor was Barry's death. Was it random? Was his death even related to what was going on with Cinnamon? All of it had become confusing.

But I knew who wasn't the author of confusion. I slipped out of bed and prayed for a long time.

By the time Amos made his way to the shower, I was the one ordering breakfast today. As I poured coffee into the mugs, he shuffled up beside me.

"You beat me out of bed today."

I set the carafe on the table and plopped down in the seat. "I couldn't sleep. Too anxious about Cinnamon. Do you think Jack is really going to have something to share with us this morning?"

Amos stabbed his fork into the fluffy scrambled eggs. "He sounded optimistic. If Jack found the private investigator, whatever he has may stop all this chaos."

I crossed my arms, feeling raised goosebumps on my flesh. "I sure hope so. Last night made me feel uneasy, especially with Cinnamon accusing her own daughter. That relationship was already on thin ice."

Amos took a swig of orange juice before responding. "I know you want this solved. It's why I reached out to Jack and have been persistent about him helping us. With his deep connections, I feel like he has something we can work with, or at least be able to pass on to the police."

"True," I thought. After the mirror message and the car crash, the police had to believe Cinnamon's life was in danger.

We finished breakfast and headed out. Soon we arrived in front of the Blue Note Lounge which looked entirely different in the sunlight. The brick building seemed like any other boring building, not a place for good food and music. But I was calling it a juke joint.

With this being our third time, the Blue Note Lounge almost felt like visiting an old friend when we walked inside. The atmosphere was so different in the daytime versus the lively nights filled with music and laughter. Smells of stale beer and chicken hung in the air, making my stomach churn.

"Feels strange being here when it's so quiet, doesn't it?" Amos whispered.

"Sure does," I agreed. It actually felt rather creepy despite the sun rays streaming through windows.

We spotted Jack sitting at a table near the back with a mug in his hand. He waved us over. "Morning, Eugeena. Amos. Coffee?"

We both accepted a cup of coffee, even though we had coffee at the hotel. Jack went in the back and returned with two steaming mugs. My heart raced as I clutched my coffee mug, eager for any bit of information that could help our dear friend.

"So, what have you got for us?" Amos asked. "Did you find the private detective?"

Jack smiled, "I did. He's right here." He gestured toward a man who seemed to float out of the shadows. I wasn't sure if he'd been there the whole time and we didn't see him or if he'd just walked into the Blue Note. Then I noticed there was another cup on the table.

The private detective stepped forward and pulled out a chair. "Good morning, folks."

I'd seen him before somewhere. He appeared younger than I would have thought. His full beard and rumpled suit needed some proper grooming. As he sat down, I noticed the callused fingertips of his left hand, evidence of a guitarist.

"Name's Derek Parker," he introduced himself, nodding at Amos and me.

I raised an eyebrow. "You wouldn't happen to be related to Cinnamon's former guitar player, Nate Parker."

The young man nodded. "Yes, my uncle Nate taught me how to play the guitar. I hung around the band and played poker on the weekend with Barry and Jack here. I also grew up with Lotus," he added, almost shyly.

I thought to myself, *Lotus has a secret admirer.* Then I remembered. "Wait, you were at the funeral yesterday talking to Lotus."

"Yes. Small world. It's nice to meet you."

Amos was ready to get down to business. "Were you able to find out any information for Barry about Cinnamon's finances?"

"From what I've gathered," Derek said as he pulled out his phone. "It looks like Cinnamon was transferring money herself."

A heavy silence settled over us like a thick blanket. I didn't for a moment believe Cinnamon had been the root cause of all her troubles. That made little sense.

"What does that mean? Did she have two bank accounts?"

Derek held up his phone and showed us an app. "Are you familiar with apps like Venmo or Cash App?"

I nodded. "Yes, my daughter likes to use those. She had me sign up for one of those a few years ago. Pay App. I only use it when she needs help with something. She doesn't like me writing checks."

Derek grinned. "A lot of young people prefer to do everything online."

Amos had been listening as we went back and forth about online accounts. He asked, "So let me get this straight. You're saying someone had been transferring money from Cinnamon's bank account over to some online account? It must have been in small increments."

"Yes." Derek confirmed while he pulled up something that had a lot of numbers on his phone.

It was so tiny on his phone, it hurt my eyes to try to view it.

He explained, "This happened over at least six to seven months. They wouldn't have been noticeable with all the other automated bill payments that have been set up. It was fifty dollars, a hundred dollars and the maximum amount moved over would be five hundred dollars. "But five hundred dollars every week over six to seven months becomes a significant amount."

Jack added. "Not Barry's style. He was old school; he pre-ferred not to deal with those online apps. I don't like them either. He and I both had conversations about keeping cash on us. Though the way of the world is debit cards, credit cards and online apps."

"Could you tell if someone had access to her accounts?" I inquired.

Derek shook his head. "It was a personal bank account. Barry told me he had access to it, but it was mainly to transfer money like payments from the gigs into her account."

"Jared has been missing," Amos pointed out. "As her current manager, maybe he was given access to the account to help his grandmother out."

Derek said. "There's no evidence that she officially added him to the account."

"But," I added, "she freely gave her password to him to do things like check her emails. And she could be old school like me keeping passwords in a notebook. Jared could have accessed her accounts easily."

Jack rubbed his chin thoughtfully. "But what about Lotus? She's got a bone to pick with her mother, too. She could know more about where her mother kept information like that, too."

Derek frowned. "I remember being around Lotus and hearing how much she didn't get along with her mother. Most of that was being young and trying to find herself. I also know she really loved seeing her mom onstage too, she just wished that Cinnamon had been around more. Plus, her paintings and her gallery bring in good money. And Lotus doesn't have official access either."

I had to agree with Derek's comments about Lotus. She seemed well off with her own career. Derek also confirmed my suspicions. His passionate defense showed deep feelings for Lotus. I was glad someone else spoke up about their doubts.

I wasn't so naïve to think that children couldn't betray and steal from their own mother. Maybe I just didn't want to believe something like that would happen to Cinnamon.

Derek stood from the table. "Barry planned on getting with Cinnamon to see what she knew about this online account. If she wasn't familiar with online accounts, she might not have known what it was. Next steps were to investigate if maybe her accounts had been hacked. Sometimes hackers send what are called phishing emails. If you click on a link, you can inadvertently give them access to your account."

"I've heard of that. Were you able to determine a name on the account? I imagine those numbers you were showing were some type of bank statement. It would show the transfer, right?"

"Yeah. The account was created about a year ago under the name CINNY WATERS. Barry said that wasn't right because Ms. Waters preferred to use her real name, especially on official accounts."

I thought out loud, "Very few people called Cinnamon by her nickname, too." A nickname her brother had given her.

Chapter 22

Derek left, and Jack headed back into the kitchen area to get more coffee. I looked around the Blue Note Lounge and noticed the sunlight shone through the windows even stronger. It was getting closer to lunch.

Amos touched my hand. "I can tell you got a lot whirling around in that head of yours."

I tried to smile because Amos was right. "I'm trying to sort it all out." I reached in my purse and pulled out the small notebook Leesa had gifted me a few months ago. I kept notebooks around the house. I loved to collect them. Derek's reveals were actually very helpful. I jotted down all the people I'd heard using the nickname Cinny.

Tommy Howard.

Olivia Harris.

Nate Parker.

Amos peered over my shoulder at the names. "I would say Tommy seems like the most obvious suspect."

"And he's a mechanic. If he had access to Cinnamon's car, he could have cut the brake line. But why? We don't know his whereabouts during Barry's shooting. He and Niecy were backstage, but they could have left and gone outside. Still, why shoot Barry?"

"Tommy is always up for money. He doesn't strike me as a guy who knows a lot of technical stuff, but like Derek said, there are other ways to get access to someone's bank account."

"So you're thinking if Barry discovered it was him, that would have been a reason to shoot him. Tommy definitely has a bad temper. He's shown us that. And that night when we passed him and Niecy, they were arguing about something."

Amos raised his eyebrow. "You noticed that."

"Yes, I did. I was afraid when he burst into Niecy's office that they were going to continue the argument, which seemed to be about money."

Amos rubbed his chin. "There's this thing with Jared. Tommy is holding a grudge against him because of his brother's death. That grudge seems to extend to Ms. Waters. He definitely doesn't have any love for her, which makes it really suspect that he's in her band."

"Absolutely. He's a strange one. We should talk to Niecy again."

"I agree," Amos said. "You don't really think the other two are suspects."

I shook my head. "No, not really. I kind of went by who gets away with calling Cinnamon by her nickname. The only person I'd ever known to call her Cinny was her brother. There seems to be certain individuals who she doesn't mind using the old nickname. Barry being one, but he's dead. Olivia and Nate spent years by her side in the band so that's understandable. I get the impression that Cinnamon may tolerate Tommy in the band, but she may not like him referring to her in such an intimate manner."

"Makes sense seeing that the person used Cinny Waters for this online account." Amos gave me a head nod, and then said, "Put that up. Jack is coming back over here."

I shut the notebook and stuffed it back into my bag. One of the people on my list happened to be Jack's wife. With the man helping us, I didn't want him to think we suspected Olivia.

Which I didn't.

But Olivia being friends for so many years with Cinnamon, she may have been privy to other private information, too.

Jack asked, "Would you all like anything else? My kitchen staff just clocked in for work. We don't officially open for a few hours, but they can whip you up something for lunch."

I looked over at Amos, who I fully expected would want some chicken fingers, but he declined. "Oh no, that's fine. We should probably head out. You've been really helpful today." Amos lifted himself from the chair, but I patted his arm and though he raised an eyebrow at me, he sat back down.

"Sorry! Jack, I do have a few more questions."

Jack seemed to be privy to quite a bit about Cinnamon. I assumed his knowledge came from years of knowing her or being married to her former backup singer. Besides, he had a whole wall dedicated to her in the Blue Note Lounge.

I also needed to cross some other suspects off my list who, though they may not refer to Cinnamon by her nickname, they were aware of it.

"Sure, I will help as much as I can." Jack smiled, but he also looked puzzled.

"What did Lotus do that made you and Olivia suspect her of stealing money? From what I could tell, Cinnamon had been very generous to her daughter, helping her open her art gallery. And Lotus is doing very well."

Jack sighed. "You're right to question. I know I could be off-base about Lotus like Derek said. He's been in love with her most of his life, so he's a little biased."

That made me smile. "I could tell he had a thing for her."

Jack nodded. "Lotus is a grown woman now and has matured over the years. She's a fine artist. That painting over there near the stage is Lotus's rendition of her mother."

I spun around in my chair. "Oh, that's beautiful. And it captures Cinnamon's likeness so well. Surely, you can't think Lotus would mean her mother harm. That painting was done with love, not just talent."

Jack leaned back in his seat, placing his hands on his belly. "I guess I just remember Lotus's rebellious days. You know she had issues with alcohol. She's been sober for several years now, but she used to act out, drunk out of her mind and disturbed her mother's performances. Cinnamon would be so embarrassed, but she'd continue on with the show."

That saddened me that Lotus publicly let out her frustrations with her mother. But it also meant Lotus wouldn't hide behind threats and messages on mirrors either. The woman we'd seen in action didn't mind openly spewing her grievances at her mother.

"We talked to Lotus. She freely admitted that she had been horrible to her mother, but she loves her. Cinnamon has been there to support her and Jared." I shook my head. "I don't think it's Jared or Lotus. If there's one thing I've learned," I glanced over at Amos, "it's that the culprit is always someone you least expect."

Amos frowned at me. "You think someone's been playing us all along, don't you?"

I nodded. "Jack, did you know that reporter, Ben Taylor, is working on an unauthorized biography of Cinnamon?" I had a feeling whoever was Ben Taylor's source was also the culprit.

Jack raised his eyebrows. "Yeah, I know. He's been around here bothering Olivia. I had to kick him out of here one night a few weeks ago. Olivia had just finished a set and was trying to get backstage. He was determined to know why Olivia left the band. Though she had a falling out with Cinnamon, Olivia is not a woman to go blabbing her mouth off, especially to some reporter. Have you met him?"

I filled Jack in on Ben Taylor calling my aunt and saying how he'd left a message back home on our phone. "He seemed really keen on exploring Cinnamon's past and her brother's death, which she had nothing to do with."

Jack waved his hands. "Ben Taylor is all washed up. He's been trying to make a name for himself for twenty years. Cinnamon isn't the first artist he's tried to make money off. I hear the only reason he's allowed to still work at the news station is because the head of the station is an old friend. But one day Ben Taylor is going to be put out to pasture. He's way past his prime and the business has changed around him."

I could see that. There was a desperation about the reporter that Amos and I witnessed yesterday. "I'm wondering if there's something in Cinnamon's past that someone is trying to make her pay for, maybe something that Ben Taylor finds fascinating enough to include in his tell-all book."

Jack frowned. "I have no idea. Cinnamon has always been a good and generous person. I can't imagine someone holding a grudge against her. Now, I know the rumors. People think there's this big conflict between my wife and Cinnamon, but there isn't. It still bothers Olivia with how fast and sudden Cinnamon reacted. Yesterday, when I talked to Nate Parker, her old guitar player, I could tell the way Cinnamon treated him really hurt him, too. But neither of them hold grudges. If anything, they're concerned."

"I almost forgot. I met Nate yesterday after the funeral. He mentioned something about a song that upset Cinnamon. I think there might be a clue there."

"How does that help us?" Amos questioned.

I explained, "I don't know, but he told me that song choice triggered his exit from the band. Must have been something about the song that set Cinnamon off."

"Let's find out." Jack pulled out his phone and scrolled through his contacts.

I couldn't help but feel a thrill of anticipation. This could be the missing piece we needed to unravel this whole mess.

Within moments, Jack dialed a number, and we all waited for an answer.

A familiar voice responded. "Hello." His voice sounded as if we'd woken him from sleep.

"Hey, Nate. It's Jack from the Blue Note. Listen, I've got Eugeena and Amos Jones here. You may have met them yesterday at Cinnamon's house. Old friends of hers. Eugeena needs some information about that song you wanted to play that upset Cinnamon? I'm going to put you on speakerphone if that's okay."

Jack placed his phone on the table and hit the speakerphone button.

"Ah, yeah," Nate's voice crackled through the phone. "Good morning or maybe good afternoon. You know after talking to you yesterday, I had an epiphany."

Jack's bushy eyebrows shot up. "What kind of epiphany?"

Nate sighed into the phone as if in pain. "I don't know why my old brain didn't understand the significance, but Cinnamon stopped singing "Cry Me a River" after Diana died."

I don't know why, but a chill ran down my spine as I asked, "Diana. Diana Hemingway?"

Nate confirmed, "Yes, it occurred to me last night that Cinny was probably upset with me for suggesting the song. She never really got over Diana's death. They were the three musketeers, right, Jack? Well, that was until..."

Jack looked thoughtful, but moved his head. Like he realized Nate couldn't see him, he stuttered out, "Yes, yes. Cinnamon, Olivia and Diana. They were quite the threesome. But why that song? Refresh an old man's mind."

"You know there was a time when Cinny didn't mind a little healthy competition. Olivia and Diana would get a chance to sing a song during Cinny's set to give her a break. Sometimes they sang the same songs. Diana had a beautiful voice and really she could rival Cinny's pipes. Jack, do you remember Diana's very last performance? This would have been before you purchased and remodeled the Blue Note. It was only like a couple of weeks before she died."

Jack's eyes opened wide. "Oh yeah." He looked over at me and Amos. "That was a very awkward evening. Cinny had a hard time coming back on stage."

I tilted my head to the side. "Cry Me a River" was sung by Ella Fitzgerald. It's about a man breaking a woman's heart."

Jack raised an eyebrow. "Yep. Diana's heart was broken."

A conversation only a few days ago came to mind. "Oh my goodness." I touched Amos's arm. "Niecy mentioned Barry and her mother used to be together."

"That's right." Jack nodded. "I told Barry at the time that was a bad idea. Even if Cinnamon kicked him to the side, Diana was her backup singer."

Nate had a coughing fit on the phone. With a strained voice he said, "It was awful when they were dating, but after Barry broke up with her, all of us felt the pain. And a few weeks later, after Diana died, we didn't know if we would ever play together again. Anyway, I wish I could apologize to Cinny, but I know she wouldn't want to hear from me. I tried to talk to her yesterday. With Barry gone, you know it's just good to clear the air with people sometimes. You just never know when your time is next."

Jack looked solemn. "You're right about that, my friend." He looked at me to see if I had anything else to say.

"Thank you, Nate," I said. "You've been very helpful. Get some rest now, okay?"

"Sure thing, Eugeena." And with that, the line went dead.

"Did that help?" Amos asked, his eyes searching my face for answers.

"Maybe," I murmured, lost in thought. "There's a connection here. I can feel it."

"That's what you are getting from the song?" Jack pressed, clearly intrigued.

"Perhaps," I replied vaguely. "We should leave. Thank you again for your time." I wanted to guard my growing theory until after Amos and I left the Blue Note.

"Alright," Jack conceded. "But if you need any more help, just let me know."

As we left the Blue Note Lounge, the sun shone brightly on the parking lot.

It wasn't until we were in the car that I turned to Amos. "I should have put another person on my list." I dug down in my bag and pulled out my notebook. Finding my pen, I wrote, "Niecy Hemingway."

Amos peered at my notebook. "Why Niecy? She seems like a good woman. Cinnamon took her in after her mother's death and I could tell she's grateful to Cinnamon. I have to say she seems to be there for Cinnamon more than her own daughter."

"I could be overthinking. I'm sure Cinnamon may just really miss her friend. That would be a perfectly valid reason for not wanting to sing and play a song for almost ten years." I sighed. "But I hate to admit that the old reporter has me thinking. He hinted that there were unexplained deaths in Cinnamon's past."

Amos' eyes widened as if a lightbulb went off in his head. "We need to learn more about how Niecy's mom died."

"Absolutely."

I just hoped the truth didn't leave me shattered by Cinnamon's involvement.

Chapter 23

We left the Blue Note Lounge and headed toward Niecy's salon. My mind replayed various events this past week. Tommy seemed like an obvious suspect because of the young man's brashness, and he certainly had no love for Jared and Cinnamon.

"Amos, that night backstage after Cinnamon's concert, what else could Niecy and Tommy be arguing about?"

Amos replied. "Well, we know from the way he came into her office, the obvious answer is they were fighting about money. He wanted to get paid." Amos slowed and stopped for a red light. He turned to look at me. "You think there's more to it?"

"Maybe," I said. "Do we know where Tommy and Niecy were when Barry got shot?"

Amos kept moving once the light turned green. "That's a good question. I will say this and I don't know why it occurred to me, but most of the band members, including Cinnamon, all looked different."

I stretched my eyes. "They'd changed clothes. So if someone shot Barry, they could have removed the clothes with the gunshot residue."

"Exactly." Amos mused, "Also, when I was riding down from the cafeteria with the coffee, I noticed Tommy was up and down the halls like he was on edge."

Did Tommy shoot Barry?

Instead of heading back to the hotel like last time, Amos found a parking garage. Before we exited the car, I had to get out what was on my mind. "There's something else. When I talked to Niecy after Barry's funeral, for a few seconds I felt like she knew exactly where Jared was. She wouldn't leave his side at the hospital. I can't believe that she was that concerned about him and that she would have left him alone when she knew he was upset."

"We'll find out shortly about what else Niecy knows."

As we rounded the corner, the familiar neon sign of Niecy's nail salon came into view. But the sign wasn't lit up. Instead, a simple "closed" sign hung in the window. I peered down and narrowed my eyes to read the hours listed on the door. "This is odd. She should have had the salon open an hour ago. And it's a Saturday, an excellent day for business."

"Let's try the door," Amos suggested. "Maybe she's in there stocking supplies or something."

I looked around, and then took a deep breath as Amos reached for the door handle. He shook it, but it was locked.

We both looked at each other, unsure what to do next. Then a sudden movement in the shadows caught my attention. "Amos, someone is in there."

Amos nodded, "I can see." He cupped his hands against the window, but then both Amos and I jumped back from the door.

Tommy's face appeared at the window, his menacing eyes glared at us.

What in the world was Tommy doing inside Niecy's salon? Was Niecy in there too? Seeing that he was still high on our suspect list, I doubted we should try to talk to him. We stepped back as Tommy unlocked the door. I was a little hesitant to step inside, but Amos and I were together. Hopefully, the young man wouldn't try anything with two seniors. Amos might look like he could be taken, but I was pretty sure his law enforcement training, though rusty, would kick in.

Lord, help us!

The salon was dark except for a light in the back, which I knew was Niecy's office.

As if he could sense the questions in my head, he stated. "Niecy isn't here. We were supposed to meet this morning, but I can't find her."

"Where could she be?" Amos queried.

I offered, "Maybe she had to pick up some supplies? But wouldn't she normally be open and have her employees run the salon until she returned?"

"I don't know." Tommy shrugged. "I don't ask her how she's running her business. She doesn't ask about mine."

I nodded, "You're a mechanic. I guess you know a lot about cars."

Tommy stared at me. "How do you know I'm a mechanic?"

"Niecy mentioned it earlier this week. We figured you all didn't do music full time."

Tommy nodded. "No, the music gig doesn't pay very well. At least not in the last few months. But my shop is a few blocks from here. I own it with my cousins."

Amos asked, "Did you all ever figure out the money problems?"

Tommy sighed deeply and shoved his hands into his jeans pocket. "I haven't heard anything. Niecy was supposed to find out after the funeral yesterday. I'm thinking she knows more than she's saying."

Here we were suspecting Tommy and he suspects Niecy of something. I eyed Tommy skeptically, not entirely sure whether to believe him. "You sure you don't have any idea where Niecy could be? It's important that we find her."

Tommy's hardened face suddenly appeared tired and worn out. He rubbed his hands down his face. "If I knew where she was, I'd tell you. I need to find her myself." He paused, then added hesitantly, "I think... I think she took my gun."

"Your gun?" Amos and I echoed each other.

"Yeah," Tommy nodded. "I showed it to Niecy a few weeks ago. She seemed interested, even though she said she hated guns. I didn't think much of it at the time, but ... Let's just say I needed to find it last night. It was gone." His voice trailed off. "She's been acting strange for a while now, too. Something must be in the water between her, Jared and Cinny."

I guess it wasn't our place to ask him what he needed his gun for. Besides, it still alarmed me he'd admitted to us he thought Niecy had it. And why would she need a gun?

Amos asked, "What do you mean by strange?"

Apparently, my mind was speeding a million miles an hour ahead of Amos. Strange to me was Niecy had a gun. The sweet-natured woman that Cinnamon thought so much of.

Tommy shrugged. "She's just secretive, like she has something going on. She's not at her apartment. So, I figured she would be here."

"If you see her, let her know we were looking for her." Amos said. He practically pushed me out the door. It wasn't like I was planning on staying.

We left the salon, both of us moving fast. Once we were half a block away, I asked. "So, how do you think he had access to the salon? And what if Niecy had been in her office hurt or something?"

Amos took out a handkerchief and rubbed his forehead. "I don't know. But why would he mention his gun was missing? It seemed really odd for him to just blurt that out to us. He came off rather hard and thuggish the past few times we've seen him, but I sensed he's genuinely worried about his gun missing."

We trekked back to the garage. By the time we'd reached the car, both Amos and I were huffing and puffing. Amos pressed the key fob to open the doors. He started up the rental car, but the air conditioning wasn't coming out fast enough for me.

While we waited, I asked, "What if it was the same gun used to shoot Barry?"

Amos answered. "I have a feeling that's what he was worried about."

My phone buzzed in my purse, and I quickly fished it out.

It felt like my heart skipped a beat when I saw the text was from Cinnamon. There was nothing the car's vents could do to ease my rising panic as I re-read the text again.

I know where Jared is now. I'm going to get him.

"Cinnamon just sent me a text. She knows where Jared is, and she's going after him!"

"Are you serious?" Amos asked, his eyes widening in alarm. "Where is he?"

"I don't know," I admitted. "She didn't say."

I texted as I tried to catch my breath. It's amazing that my fingers actually worked, although I ended up typing the letter U instead of you. That was something I fussed at my own kids about, not using English.

Cinnamon, where are u?

237

Amos guided the car out of the garage. "Any luck?"

"None. I've got this feeling in my gut, Amos. How is she getting around? Her car is totaled."

"She stayed at a hotel last night. Maybe she rented a car."

"I guess, but I figured she would be too shaky to drive. We need to find Lotus. Surely, Cinnamon wouldn't go without his mother knowing she'd found him."

"Let's find Lotus, then." Amos made a sharp right turn, and I realized he was heading back toward the gallery.

I had this crazy feeling that maybe we should just keep driving until we left this city and this whole mess behind.

Chapter 24

After we entered Lotus's art gallery, we could visibly see Lotus working with a man to position a large portrait on the wall. She looked up and noticed us but didn't appear too excited to see us. She said something to the man, and then waved for someone else to come over to help him.

She approached us with a frown. "I would have thought you two would be flying out of here by now. Haven't you had enough of my mother? I know she's ruined your vacation."

"Lotus, have you heard anything from your mother?" I asked.

"No, I haven't talked to her since yesterday when she accused me of being the one threatening her." Lotus's anger turned to concern. "What's wrong? You both look really worried."

"Your mother sent a text to me. She said she found Jared and was going to get him. Did she text you?"

"I don't know. I left my phone in the office." Lotus sprinted toward the back.

Amos and I tried to keep up with her, but my energy was already waning.

Inside her office, Lotus scanned her phone. "She texted me about an hour ago. I don't know how I missed it. Where did she say he was at?"

Amos replied, "That's the thing, she didn't say."

"We have a theory," I said. "Do you know where else Niecy would be? She's supposedly not at her salon. It's closed, and she's not at her apartment."

"Niecy?" Lotus questioned, her expression turning to one of confusion. "Why would she know anything?"

"Well, we think she may be more involved in this whole situation than we originally suspected," Amos explained.

Lotus furrowed her brow, deep in thought. Then her face darkened. "Mom is always telling me to give Niecy a break. That girl is sneaky. What do you think she did to Jared?"

I shook my head. "We don't know, but yesterday when I asked her if she'd found Jared, I felt like she knew where he was hiding out."

Lotus's face turned grim. "Niecy inherited her mother's house after she passed away. It's out in the countryside, a bit far from the city, which is why she usually stays at her rental apartment."

"Lotus, I need you to call the police," Amos asked. "Tell them everything we know and make sure they understand we're headed to Niecy's mother's house."

"Alright, I'll do it," Lotus said, "but I'm going with you. If Niecy had anything to do with Jared going missing, and if she's the one that has been messing with my mother this whole time, she has to deal with me."

I didn't like the sound of that. I looked over at Amos, who looked just as concerned.

We hadn't told Lotus that Tommy suspected Niecy took his gun.

"Lotus, you really should stay behind," Amos insisted as we all stood outside our rental car. Amos ended up being the one to dial the cops. He'd specifically asked for the detectives on Cinnamon's case.

"Absolutely not," Lotus screeched. "I'm going with you. Jared is my son, and I'll do whatever it takes to protect him." She crossed her arms over her chest, her eyes daring either of us to challenge her.

I certainly didn't envy Cinnamon having to raise this child.

"Besides," she said, leaning forward with her fingers pointing toward both of us. "You won't be able to find the place without me."

We needed her help, whether we liked it or not. I knew Lotus was worried sick about her son, and I couldn't blame her. It was a complicated situation, and I just hoped that we'd be able to find Jared and Cinnamon in time to stop whatever sinister plan was unfolding.

"Fine," I sighed, giving in. "Let's go then. We need to find them soon."

We piled into the car. Lotus guided Amos as he drove through the winding roads.

"Your mother's been taking care of this house for Niecy?" I asked, trying to break the tension.

"Yeah, she has," Lotus replied. "When Niecy turned eighteen, Mama gave her the keys as a birthday present. I've been in there only a few times since Diana died, but nothing much has changed. Niecy has kept the place the same all these years and my mother certainly didn't touch it."

Thinking about what Nate said earlier about the song, I asked Lotus, "So you remember Diana?"

Lotus nodded, and for the first time, smiled. "Yes, Diana was such fun. She was a lot sillier than my mom and Olivia.

But, man, could she sing. She could hit those high notes like nobody else. I remember Niecy when she was born. Diana's pride and joy. Diana spent every moment with Niecy. She even sang onstage with that girl on her hip."

"There's a picture at the Blue Note Lounge with Cinnamon holding you. Do you remember how old you were?"

Lotus was quiet for a second in the back seat. Finally, she answered, "I think I was three or four. You know it's hard to remember those ages. Barry told me later, when I asked about the photo, that he'd taken it. He always tried to remind me how much my mother loved me, even though she had a hard time saying it."

"Where we were from, we probably never heard our own parents say they loved us either." I commented. "Later, when I got older, I realized their love was in the meals and how they took care of us."

No one spoke again until Lotus mentioned an upcoming road where Amos would need to take a right. As the car jostled over a rough patch of road, I couldn't help but hope the police arrived before we did. I did not know what we would find. This trip could be a complete waste of time. That made me sad because Amos's and my time was winding up here in Nashville. I felt in many ways that we hadn't enjoyed our stay.

"Almost there," Lotus murmured, more to herself than us. We navigated a final bend, and the house came into view. An inviting farmhouse structure nestled among trees.

Amos pulled into the driveway, which was occupied by another car. "Lotus, do you recognize the vehicle in the front?"

"No, I don't.

A sticker on the back of the car matched the same rental company that we were using. "We thought Cinnamon rented a car last night, so that could be it."

"Looks quiet," Amos muttered under his breath. "Too quiet. Maybe we should wait for the police."

"No, if Niecy has Jared and my mom in there, then let's go." Lotus was outside the car before I could get my hand on the door handle. I looked at Amos, who had the most exasperated expression on his face.

He grumbled. "We should have left that woman back at her gallery."

I agreed with him, but I knew Lotus wanted to find her son. Jared had been missing for the past four days.

We approached the house. My legs were feeling heavy with every step, and I had an urge to turn around. The house needed a coat of paint, and while it didn't appear like the structure was going to fall down on us, the surrounding landscape desperately needed Amos's lawnmower and landscaping skills. A once-vibrant garden lay neglected, its plants overgrown and wild.

"Remember," Amos said, his voice firm and steady. "We're in this together. We'll find Jared and Cinnamon. Police shouldn't be that far out."

Before we could even reach the door, the front door swung open. Niecy stepped out to greet us. "I was wondering when you all were coming. Come on in."

I hesitated, grabbing Amos's hand. He squeezed my hand, but didn't turn to look at me. I was pretty sure his eyes were on the gun that Niecy had pointed in our direction.

Chapter 25

Lotus sucked in a breath behind us, but for once she didn't pop off and say anything. I'd wondered why Lotus took such a dislike to this girl. What was it Lotus said?

That girl is sneaky.

Cinnamon may have found her own daughter exasperating, but the artistic observation for details that Lotus had should not have been questioned. Her intuition had been spot on.

"Niecy," Amos said gently, his hands raised in a gesture of surrender. "We just want to find Jared and Cinnamon. No one wants to hurt you."

"You came to the right place." She spat, her grip tightening on the gun. "Get in here so I can figure out what to do with all of you."

One by one, we moved past her. My eyes connected with hers because I didn't want to see that gun up close. The floorboards creaked as we all huddled in the small foyer.

"Listen to me," Amos asked. "I've already called the cops. They're on their way. Put the gun down, Niecy. Let us help you make things right."

My throat felt tight. Even when faced with danger, Amos never backed down from his former cop mode.

As we stood there, locked in that tense standoff, I couldn't help but reflect on how our honeymoon had come to this. I should have shared with Amos my brief thought about leaving Nashville. He probably would have gladly agreed.

Niecy waved the gun around. "Move into the living room. That's where Jared and Cinnamon are."

We all shuffled into a dated living room that somehow remained cozy. But the decor didn't matter as I caught sight of Cinnamon sitting on the couch, cradling Jared's limp form in her arms. His breathing sounded shallow, and it was clear he needed help — fast. What had Niecy done to him? He looked like he was on drugs. Nothing like the young man I'd seen only four nights ago.

Cinnamon looked up at us, her eyes wide and red-rimmed, but there was a fierce determination in them too.

"Jared," Lotus gasped, rushing to her son's side. She touched his forehead. "We need to get him to a hospital."

Niecy shook her head so hard she looked like a bobblehead doll. "No one is going anywhere. Both of you get over there, I want to see all of you together."

Amos grabbed my elbow and hustled me over to where Cinnamon sat on the couch. I sat beside her while Amos stood.

Cinnamon looked at me. "I'm so sorry to get y'all into this. I had no idea."

Niecy yelled, "Stop talking! I can't think!"

So we didn't talk. No one said a word. I strained my ears like I thought Amos was probably doing, waiting to hear police sirens.

But none came.

The only sound was Niecy pacing up and down making the floorboards creak under her feet.

I'd read a crime novel recently that described a sociopath as having the ability to mask their true self. They could look pretty normal. Until Nate explained only a few hours ago how that song choice affected Cinnamon and the reason, Niecy seemed like a really sweet girl to me. But no matter how well people think they are hiding true intentions, something will slip out.

My years of working around students for thirty years, I could tell so much about a child from their body language. So while I was shocked, I wasn't that surprised that Niecy would show her true self. The person behind those threats, who would kill a person by cutting their brake line, was very smart, but also a coward.

Finally, I couldn't take it anymore. "Could you kindly tell us why you are doing this? You've obviously been angry with Cinnamon, and I suspect Barry, for a while. Maybe about a year ago this all started for you."

Niecy stopped pacing and looked at me. Then at Amos. Her eyes finally strayed toward Cinnamon. She pointed the gun, "She's a murderer. Her and Barry. She shouldn't be here."

Amos asked, his hand on my shoulder. I knew he didn't want me to talk anymore, but I couldn't help myself. "So is that the gun you used to kill Barry?"

She looked down at the gun as though she didn't recognize her own hand. "It wasn't supposed to happen like that. I went outside and heard Jared arguing with Barry. I overhead Barry tell Jared he hired a private investigator. Barry was so determined to prove his innocence. When Cinny fired him, he should have just gone on. But he didn't. I should have known. Cinny and Barry. Binny shall we call them. You know how couples like to combine their names. They have been messing up people's lives forever."

"What are you talking about, Niecy?" Cinnamon asked. "If you are mad with me, why did you do this to Jared?"

Niecy shouted, "Because you love him. Probably love him more than your own daughter. I could never get anything over on Lotus like I could with Jared. He is so trusting."

"You heifer!" Lotus shouted.

Niecy leveled her gun at Lotus. "Don't you dare. You've always looked down on me. Your own mother murdered my mother."

We all frowned, spun our heads around looking at each other.

Cinnamon spoke first, "That's not true. Though I will say that I have felt guilty."

Niecy shouted. "Felt guilty! You are guilty. Barry was with my mother and she loved him. But no, Barry had to break up with her because his heart was for Cinny. You, sinful woman. My mother was heartbroken when she got in that car. It's your fault she crashed. And Barry's."

Cinnamon's chest heaved. "Barry and I had been on and off with our relationship long before your mother started as a backup singer for me. She knew when she started dating him that Barry was a man who cherished his bachelorhood. He'd broken up with her weeks before the crash."

"But then she saw you two. The betrayal." Niecy stepped forward. "You knew how she felt. How depressed she was, and you carried on anyway."

Lotus spoke up. "No one in this room is a saint. I remember that night. Diana had been drinking and my mom tried to stop her from getting into her car."

Cinnamon glanced over at Lotus, her eyes glimmering with tears. "Yes, I did. We all tried to stop her. She slumped in that chair like she was sleeping. Next thing we knew, she'd slipped out. If we could have stopped her, we would have."

Niecy's hand, and eventually her entire arm, shook as she held the gun. "I always looked up to you, but you're nobody to look up to. You said yourself you felt guilty for my mother dying. You were even guilty of your brother's death too."

Cinnamon sucked in a breath. "What?"

Niecy smiled.

It was by far the ugliest smile I had ever seen on a person. And she was a pretty girl.

She continued. "I read your journal. It's how I found out how you felt guilty about my mother's death. You felt guilty about your brother's death, too. You caused that fight to happen. If your brother wasn't defending your honor... Charlie, that's his name. He would be alive today."

I don't know who gasped, me or Cinnamon. Maybe both of us because Amos gripped my shoulder.

Cinnamon's body shook. "You are so evil. I know you miss your mama, but she would not have wanted you to turn out like this."

Niecy kept that ugly smile pasted on her face. "Well, I guess we will never know. Thanks to you! I guess you felt sorry for what you did. That's why you took me into your home."

In the distance, sirens could be heard. My body wanted to relax in relief, but this child still had a gun and was spewing out such hatred. I couldn't imagine how she walked around the way she did with all that pent up anger. Somehow she had gotten hold of Cinnamon's journal and it triggered something inside of her.

Niecy's smile slipped from her face as her eyebrows furrow. She turned her head toward the door. Perhaps it finally dawned on her that sirens were approaching her house. Whatever it was, the split second of distraction was a godsend.

I don't know who sprang into action first. I bet it was Amos. He threw something that looked like a big round paperweight. I don't know when he grabbed it or how long he had it in his hand, but he hit the young woman square in her nose. She grabbed her nose and stumbled backwards. And although she didn't fall, she roared with pain.

I looked at Cinnamon and lifted my feet. Seeing what I was about to do, we shoved the coffee table that separated us from Niecy on its side. The items, which included a large coffee-table book and several whatnots, became flying objects. The book spun across the floor, heading straight toward Niecy's foot. She jumped over the book, but then twisted her foot on the statue of a little girl holding an umbrella. That had her tripping forward almost losing her balance again.

That girl could not go down!

She still had the gun!

By that time, Lotus had grabbed a lamp from beside her and threw it at Niecy.

Niecy shot wildly, hitting the lamp. As the broken pieces rained down on her, she covered her head and stepped forward. But her foot connected with the coffee table book.

I almost cheered when her legs flew out from under her, but Amos grabbed me and shielded me as we went to the left. I caught sight of Cinnamon and Lotus dragging Jared with them in the opposite direction.

Amos and I ran out into the tiny foyer, but not before another shot whizzed by our heads. The girl was down on the ground screaming all kinds of expletives, but she still had the gun in her hand.

Where were the police?

I could only hope Cinnamon and Lotus could take cover and protect Jared, who still remained unconscious.

A window crashed open, spraying glass all over the living room and nearby where Niecy struggled to get her footing. She looked up, panic on her face. Someone dressed in law enforcement fatigues held a rifle, yelling at her to put the gun down.

Amos and I slumped to the floor with our hands in the air as the front door flew open. I had never prayed so hard that none of us left this place with a bullet wound.

Or worse.

In a body bag.

Chapter 26

The paramedics rushed Jared out first. In the midst of the confusion and chaos, Jared opened his eyes. He recognized his mother and grandmother, but quickly went into distress. Lotus rode in the ambulance with her son and we promised to meet her at the hospital. Some of us had to stay behind and give statements.

It appeared as if Niecy had been drugging Jared. But why? There were so many questions the girl needed to answer. With two law enforcement agents flanking each side, they led Niecy out with handcuffs. She looked like we'd beat her up, though none of us touched her. Well, not physically. Between the paperweight and the lamp, she had bruises and scratches on her face. She seemed to limp when she walked, which I'm sure happened when the items from the coffee table had her sprawling across the floor.

She stared daggers at all of us as she passed.

All I could think about was how Cinnamon had helped this child after her mother died. She had a successful business and had a foot in the music business. It would all be thrown away. Surely she had to have known her mother wouldn't have wanted that for her.

The police escorted the rest of us back to a small dining room area where the detectives waited for us. Detective Harris looked at all of us as though we were as crazy as Niecy. But there was some admiration on his face as well as he asked, "So all of you took her down?"

"Well, it was four against one." I said.

"But she had a gun," he said incredulously.

Amos answered for all of us. "So you expected us to just sit there so she could use one or all of us as targets? Y'all took your time getting here."

"Exactly," I huffed.

Cinnamon looked at both of us, and then at the detective. "Please ask your questions and let Eugeena and Amos go. They're in Nashville on their honeymoon, and I have completely ruined the week for them."

I patted Cinnamon's hand. "We're fine. But today is our last day in Nashville. I'm just glad this has all settled for you." I looked at the detective. "At least I hope so. You do have some evidence."

Amos spoke up. "I bet that gun Niecy had was used to shoot Barry. She practically confessed that she was worried he'd been on to her as the one stealing the money."

Detective Harris nodded. "Don't worry, we will get her. She's going to face a lot of charges come Monday morning. In the meantime, she will stew in a jail cell the rest of the weekend. Sit tight. We will release you soon."

After the detective left, Cinnamon cleared her throat. "I would have never thought it was her. She lived with me for years at my old house. It was the same house where I raised Lotus, so she moved into Lotus's old room. I always thought that's why Lotus resented her so much. I have been wrong about so many things."

"So what happened almost a year ago?" I asked. "Something triggered her."

Cinnamon shook her head. "Niecy had some work done at her apartment, so I told her she could stay with me. I'd just bought that new house and, to be honest, it was beautiful but lonely. I was happy for the company."

"So did you just have your journal lying around?"

Cinnamon sighed. "I'd been seeing a therapist. This getting old is something. Some things I used to keep squared away in a corner would bother me mercilessly. So I started journaling and when I moved into the new house, I guess I just got into the habit of leaving the journal on my nightstand, sometimes on the bed." She blew out a breath, an incredulous look on her face. "All those years she stayed with me, I never knew Niecy to invade my privacy though."

"People get nosy about different things. Probably at the time it was innocent and she was just tempted." A thought came to me, so I asked, "So she stayed with you the night Barry was shot?"

Cinnamon frowned. "Yes, she did. I thought it was unusual at first because she hadn't stayed over since moving back into her apartment. I assumed she just was concerned about me and that she also wanted the company. We talked about Barry that night. She didn't give me any hints that she'd hurt him."

Amos asked. "She'd changed clothes though."

I snapped my fingers. "That's right! Why didn't I think of that?"

Cinnamon thought for a moment. "Of course. She was wearing a black dress onstage, but ..." She gulped. "At the hospital she had on a t-shirt and jeans. But still, she's young and she would have changed out of her clothes. I've seen her do that after other performances." She stopped talking as reality set in. "You know, even after what we just saw, I'm having trouble believing it. Where would she get a gun? She's never liked them."

"Before we came here, Tommy was looking for her. He said she showed interest in his gun, and then it went missing."

Cinnamon gasped. "So was he in on everything with her?"

Amos shook his head. "I don't know. She may have been using him for her purposes. I bet you she learned a thing or two from Tommy about cars."

Cinnamon held her hands to her chest. "Learned enough to cut my brakes. Do you think that's the real reason she stayed with me that night? You know she was the first one at the hospital after my accident. That child wanted me dead over something I had no control over." She began to cry, wiping tears as they fell.

I got up and reached for some paper towels, and then looked in the fridge. Niecy had packed it with bottled water and some deli food. Apparently, Niecy seemed to make sure Jared ate food and drank water. I took out three bottled waters and sat back down.

Cinnamon wiped her face and took a gulp of water. "We argued that night. Diana had a tendency to drink when she was upset and she could be ugly. She was furious with Barry and me. We tried to take her keys, but she lied and told us she would sit and let the alcohol wear off. Even though she left on her own, I still felt guilt and so did Barry."

We sat quietly trying to soak everything in. I could see Niecy reading Cinnamon's private thoughts and taking offense. But why not just talk to her? Instead, the child cooked up one scheme after the other.

Detective Harris returned, and we gave formal statements. Then he let us go. Amos drove us to Nashville General Hospital. I realized this was our third time here as the doors slid open. We found Jared's room, but Amos and I didn't go in since he had limited visitors in ICU.

Lotus came out of his room to let Cinnamon see him. Worn down with red-rimmed eyes, she looked at both of us.

"How's Jared?" I asked.

"He looks better, but he's still very weak. I don't know why she did it, but she'd been using tranquilizers on him. He's dehydrated and out of it. It's so hard seeing him with IVs hooked to his arms."

"I can understand. Has he talked at all?"

Lotus nodded. "Just a little. The last time he called me, he must have been trying to say he needed help."

I nodded. "He saw Barry get shot. Probably saw her pull the trigger. I'm sure he couldn't fathom why Niecy had shot a man thcy both supposedly loved."

"I have no doubt that he was in shock," Lotus said. "I just don't know if he went over to talk to her or if she tricked him into that house. I guess when he's fully awake, he will tell us. That's if he remembers." She sucked in a breath and held her hands to her chest. "What I know is you both saved my son's life and probably saved my mom's life, too. I know you have seen the worst between us, but I really do love my mother."

"We have no doubts. Just be sure that you talk to each other. Both of you are Jared's support system and he needs you both right now."

I waited until Cinnamon came back out. There was still a discussion we needed to have. One that I wasn't looking forward to, but I knew we needed to get it out of the way. She returned to the waiting room, exchanging places with Lotus.

Amos had gone to get coffee, so Cinnamon took the seat next to me. For once, I didn't know how to approach the question that had been on my mind since Niecy blurted it. I eased into it. "You said that you think about Charlie a lot?"

Cinnamon twisted her fingers in her hand. "Yes. I think about what it would be like if he were still alive." Her voice caught at the end of the sentence.

"You have been feeling guilty about his death because of survivor's guilt."

She shook her head. "No, it's more than that. My family left town pretty quickly after Charlie died." Her smile was wry and bitter. "I've heard through the grapevine over the years that people had many questions about Charlie's death. Niecy was right. It was my fault. I didn't tell you back then, but I had met this older guy. I have to say I lived up to my mama's accusation of being fast in the tail. She said that to me so often, and it made me feel some kind of way. Anyhow, I got pregnant, and the first person who got angry about the whole ordeal was Charlie. He knew the guy and accused him of taking advantage of me."

"Well, he did. He was older than you. I imagine you were underage for him."

Cinnamon nodded. "Yes, but I knew what I was doing. I wasn't prepared for the consequences. Charlie fought him and it wasn't a fair fight since the other guy had a knife."

"So Charlie's death had nothing to do with Bubba and that brawl that broke out after the game?"

"Honestly, Eugeena, I think Charlie used that brawl as a cover to get in some good licks on my behalf. Protect my virtue and all that. But, like I said, the older guy had a knife, probably shouldn't have even been at some high school game. Charlie was never gonna win."

Tears formed in Cinnamon's eyes. Before they could fall, I asked. "So your parents shipped you off to live with your grandmother and I'm assuming this man is Lotus's dad."

Cinnamon looked off into the distance. She answered softly. "Yes. She looks so much like him. He could draw too, so she gets her artistic side from him. As well as that temper."

"Have you ever told her?"

Cinnamon shook her head. "I've never told her because I've tried to put it behind me. My mother never forgave me for losing Charlie. Then, my grandmother was a strict, religious woman, and she helped me learn how to take care of Lotus. I never graduated from high school. I just took care of Lotus. But I was so ready to leave. When I turned eighteen, I knew Nashville was the place for me and my baby. But everything happened so fast once people heard me sing. I couldn't take a small child with me to some places where I sang."

"I imagine they weren't like the Blue Note."

Cinnamon chuckled. "Not hardly."

"So tell me, when did you meet Barry?"

A smile spread across Cinnamon's face, but tears spilled over. "We met one night after I'd sang a few sets. He told me he could make me a star, and I told him he was full of it. But he kept hanging around and I soon started liking him. The rest is history." She smirked. "You know, maybe that old reporter, Ben Taylor, does have a story to tell."

"No, he doesn't. He has no right to be in your private business. I'm going to assume that Niecy had been feeding him stories about you all this time, too. Once he sees that she's been arrested he's going to be looking really foolish."

"Thank you again, Eugeena. I owe you and Amos. I'm so sorry I have messed this week up for you."

"No worries. Amos and I were together doing what we liked to do best."

Chapter 27

The sun had barely risen when I cracked open one heavy eyelid wincing at the sliver of light slipping through the curtains. My body ached from the previous night's events. That face-off with Niecy had been something else. Amos stirred beside me, and for a moment, I was content just to watch him sleep. But we had places to be, so I gently shook his shoulder.

"Amos, honey, we gotta get up. We're leaving for Memphis today."

He groaned, rubbing his eyes before sitting up. "All right. Let's get moving."

We packed our bags in silence, the weight of last night still hanging heavy in the air. I took one last look at our home away from home for the week, checking around to make sure we hadn't left anything.

Amos packed up the rental car while I officially checked us out. I hadn't climbed inside the passenger seat good when I heard my phone ringing. Amos and I exchanged looks.

"Do you think I should just ignore this and let you get down the road?"

He shook his head. "Might as well answer it. Could be someone from back home."

I dug the phone out of my purse and saw it wasn't someone from home. I sighed, but clicked to answer.

"Hello, Cinnamon."

"Hey, Eugeena. I know you and Amos must be on the road now."

"Yes, we are heading out to Memphis now."

"I can't thank you enough for all that you did to help me. Please let Amos know how much I appreciate you both," Cinnamon said, her voice low and tired.

"I'm glad that we could help, Cinnamon. How's Jared doing? I know he's been through one ordeal after the other."

Cinnamon sighed. "Yes, Lotus and I went to visit him together. He has some rehabilitation ahead of him, but I think he's going to pull through just fine."

"That's good. I hope you take some time to heal yourself."

Cinnamon remained quiet for a while. "I wish I had known how Niecy felt or that she would have talked to me. Her mother was one of my dearest friends. Barry and I often talked about that night. Though our feelings were deep for each other, we both never forgot how Diana stormed out that night. I blamed myself. He did too. It's probably why we never married like people expected."

My heart hurt for my friend. "You did a good thing taking in Niecy and raising her. When she needed both you and Barry, neither one of you abandoned her. You are a good person, Cinnamon."

"Thank you for saying that. You know, it's been too long since I've been in Charleston. I will have to plan to visit you and Amos in the future."

"We'll be glad to have you."

"I hoped to be in Memphis next week, but I'm canceling all my gigs for the rest of the year. Lotus will help me get everyone paid from the past few gigs. Between Jared and me, we'd been struggling without Barry."

"I heard he was the glue that kept everything together. May he rest in peace."

"Amen." Cinnamon cleared her throat. "Something I failed to tell you and others is I haven't been feeling like myself. When I went to see that therapist, there was more going on with me."

When Cinnamon mentioned seeing a therapist, I wondered if whatever she was going through had caused her to feel paranoid. It was obvious that she had been pushing away and withdrawing from others. Barry noticed it and had mentioned his concerns to Lotus.

"Not that it's any of my business, but did they give you a diagnosis?"

Cinnamon was quiet for a moment. "You know my grandmother and mama both had dementia before they died. My grandmother was very paranoid."

My heart sank. "I'm so sorry, Cinnamon."

"Hey, it's better to be prepared, right? Plus, Lotus and I have a lot of talking to do. I know I haven't always been the mother she needed. I don't want to waste any more time fighting."

The revelations from last night still shook me, but also made my fond memories of Charlie Waters that much more bittersweet. He'd fought for his sister's honor. Now it appeared my friend had another battle ahead to deal with. "I hope you two will plan some counseling together. There is still time to work through everything. And you need your family. I'm praying for you both."

"Thank you. Have a safe trip. Please stay in touch when you are back home."

"Will do." I said goodbye as well and hung up the phone.

I blew out another breath. Amos had driven off as I talked. Even though he'd encouraged me to answer the phone, we had no choice but to keep going. Our time in Nashville had ended.

And what a time we had.

Amos and I talked about what parts we should share with family when we got back and what should stay between us. I could see my children never wanting me to leave town again. I got into enough trouble back home.

The drive to Memphis was long, but the open road gave us time to reflect and process everything that had happened. It was as if the car became a sanctuary, a space where Amos and I could share our thoughts.

"All of this could have been avoided if the child had only sat down and talked to Cinnamon and Barry."

Amos nodded. "I agree. But when she felt like those two were responsible for her mother's death, the rage of it took over more than the logic."

"Cinnamon loved Barry, but with Niecy's mom getting upset about what she perceived as Barry's betrayal..." I shook my head. "There's no going back after a life has been lost. So much tragedy."

"Well, Niecy will have time to sit in a jail cell and think through some of her choices too." Amos added.

"Do you think Cinnamon and her family are safe?"

Amos looked at me. "Oh yeah. Niecy is definitely going to go down, probably for first degree murder for Barry. She has attempted murder for Jared. And... well, it could have been bad for Cinnamon, Lotus and us."

I gulped. "I'm glad you could keep her talking until the cops got there, but when the gun went off," I shuddered, "I just knew she'd killed someone else."

I could still feel the whizz of a bullet passing us.

Thank you, Lord!

We sat in silence and at some point, I dozed off.

When we arrived in Memphis, we took some much needed rest for the day.

I was glad we did because the sweltering heat of Memphis pressed down on us as we navigated the bustling crowds on Beale Street. Colorful signs adorned the tops of buildings and the air buzzed with excitement. This was how it was when we first arrived in Nashville, at the beginning of our trip. While it was a different city, I was grateful for the do over of sorts.

We spent three nights in a row listening to music and doing as much dancing as our old bodies would allow.

With only a few days left, Amos and I enjoyed a scrumptious dinner of chicken and ribs at B.B. King's Blues Club.

"Amos, can I be honest?" I asked, locking eyes with him as he cleaned off a rib.

"Always."

"Next time you plan a trip, make sure it's somewhere where we don't know anyone. In fact, let's go somewhere far away. Out of the country, maybe."

He glanced at me, and his eyes lit up with amusement. Then he threw his head back and laughed until tears ran down his face. I laughed right along with him, a sweet relief lifting my spirit.

Amos wiped his eyes with a napkin. "That sounds like a fine idea, Eugeena. Believe me, that's been on my mind too. I'm just glad you're willing to travel again."

I grinned, "Amos, wherever you go, I'm going. You can count on it."

Epilogue

Amos and I returned to Sugar Creek in the early morning hours. I almost could've kissed the ground here in South Carolina when our plane landed. Not to be cliché, but there was no place better in the world than the place one called home. I slept like I hadn't the entire time we'd been gone. Our bed felt as good as any hotel room.

We probably would have stayed in bed longer, but the doorbell rang. Leesa dropped off our furry bundle of joy. Porgy and I hadn't been separated in the years that he'd come to live with me. While I knew he enjoyed being with my grandkids, I could tell by the way he tore across *his* yard that he was also happy to be back home.

I unpacked and did laundry, and then spent much of the day in the kitchen. One of my favorite past times was baking, and I was in the mood for lemon pound cake. Knowing how my family liked to eat, I whipped up enough batches for three loaves. After taking the cakes out of the oven, I grabbed a glass of sweet iced tea and walked out onto my front porch.

I had missed my rocking chair. The breeze was a bit muggy, but the overhead fans and the cold iced tea made it tolerable. I peered around my neighborhood, watching folks arrive from work for the day. I waved at a few people walking by.

I hadn't heard from Cinnamon since we'd left Nashville. I made a note to check in with her in a few days after we had settled in.

Until then, I prayed for her and her family.

A smile spread across my face as I saw a minivan approach, its shiny surface reflecting the sun's rays. My heart swelled as I set my glass of tea down and rose from my chair. Before I made it down the steps, both Kisha and Tyric came barreling toward me.

"Well, isn't this a nice surprise? There go my babies." I spread my arms wide, bracing myself for the inevitable collision.

Kisha, in her boundless energy, came running straight into my welcoming arms. "Grandma, we missed you! Did you bring us anything?"

I laughed.

My daughter rolled her eyes. "Kisha, don't be rude."

I grabbed Kisha and Tyric's hand. "It's alright. I've got a surprise for everyone. Let's head inside. Your grandpa Amos is in the back with Porgy."

I'd never felt more grateful for the normalcy of being home and enjoying my family. At least until I peeked over at my daughter's face.

Now Leesa and I had had our conflicts, but not near as intense as Cinnamon with her daughter Lotus. I could read when my only daughter had something on her mind. As she'd grown into motherhood, it really warmed my heart to see so much of me in her.

I was so proud of her and before she left today, we would take on whatever she had on her mind together.

NOTE: You can read more about what was on Leesa Patterson's mind in the novella, ***Falling For You Again*** or go to https://books2read.com/fallingforyouagain

Author's Note

Thank you for your patience! It's been almost two years since the last Eugeena Patterson Mystery, and I appreciate the emails and direct messages requesting updates about the next book. I have at least four more books I'm working on, so as long as Ms. Eugeena has amateur sleuth adventures to share, I'm more than happy to write them.

I want to thank my editor, Felicia Murrell, for helping edit the large majority of this series. Your insights and reminders are very helpful. When you get to book #6 there are a lot of details to recall.

Ever since *Deep Fried Trouble,* the first book in the series, I've kept Eugeena Patterson a homebody. That's not by accident. While I wouldn't refer to Eugeena as an introvert like me, she and I definitely have the love of our home in common. She's much better in the kitchen than me. For those of you always asking me about recipes, well, we'll see. I have had something in the works for a while.

I get to travel for my day job (not a full-time author yet) and one of my most enjoyable experiences was a conference in Nashville, Tennessee. After hours, I walked around the city exploring and was amazed at the great music blasting out of pretty much every other establishment I walked by. Most every restaurant had elements of the musicians and singers that make Nashville their home-base.

When I was thinking about locations for Eugeena and Amos to go for their honeymoon, I ran through a dozen or so places. But I kept coming back to Music City USA. The Blue Note Lounge, to my knowledge, is fictional to this book, but I'm sure there are similar places that serve up hot chicken and music. I had a blast writing about the place and kept wanting to have more scenes at the Blue Note.

In the five previous Eugeena Patterson Mysteries, I hadn't really delved into Eugeena's childhood. But I've always known her mom died when she was young and her dad raised her with the help of her aunt Esther. So as I started plotting and thinking about characters, that's where my mind went. Who did Eugeena hang out with as a child? What would she have been like as a little girl? What were some of her childhood memories?

Thus, Cinnamon Waters was birthed as a great character for Eugeena to connect with on this Nashville trip. I have quite a few childhood friends who impacted me that I've never reconnected with. Cinnamon turned out to be a much more complex character than I could ever imagine. I can see her coming back again in the future.

I had a lot of fun developing so many new characters for *A Spicy Predicament*. I hope you enjoyed them as well. For those of you who missed next-door neighbor Louise Hopkins, the twins Annie Mae and Willie Mae Brown, and so many others, don't worry, we will be returning to Sugar Creek for the next book.

Maybe it's because I live in the South, but I have pulled pork barbecue on the brain for the next book. Be sure to flip over to the next page to learn more about *Marinated Conditions*, Eugeena Patterson Mysteries, Book #7.

Marinated Conditions

Eugeena Patterson-Jones is excited about planning her daughter Leesa Patterson's wedding. With three months to go, there's lots to do. They meet for lunch at the award-winning Smokin' Ward barbecue food truck owned by Leesa's wedding caterer.

Lately the Smokin' Ward owners have been at odds with a local barbecue competitor. When the competitor's body is found inside his food truck, Leesa's friends become suspects.

Usually, Eugeena is the one who's sticking her nose into situations, but Leesa is determined to find out who's trying to destroy her friends' business and frame them for murder. The mother and daughter team up to find the smoking gun.

CHAPTER 1

I didn't have to look at my watch to know that breakfast had been a few hours ago. When it was time to eat, my body had a way of letting me know. I suddenly started thinking so hard about food, I could almost taste it. I have always had a love affair with food and mealtimes were like sharing time with an old friend. Lately, when I found myself thinking about certain types of food, fond memories accompanied those thoughts.

There was always plenty of good cooking growing up in the Lowcountry. My earliest memories are of me sitting at the kitchen table while my mama baked or prepared dinner. She seemed to cook something special every night, and not just on Sunday. I imagine it's why I spent so much time in the kitchen as an adult. It was the closest activity I had that connected me to my mama who'd passed when I was twelve years old.

Last night, my only daughter, Leesa, had brought the kids over and we'd spent time talking about her upcoming nuptials. Leesa and I have come a long way from the bickering mother and daughter to having more understanding about each other as women. I'd missed out on having my mama around when I was Leesa's age, so I truly treasured watching my baby girl. Even though she was a mother of two, the past few months I liked seeing her revert back to being that little girl who pretended her future wedding. But now it was for real. It's been a long time coming and I was really proud of this next step in her life.

From the moment her fiancé Chris Black proposed last June, Leesa dived into planning for their wedding. They'd both agreed on a full year for the engagement. Since the beginning of the year, we'd met every week for lunch and then we gathered at least one weekend a month with Leesa's besties. Hard to believe the upcoming date was a little less than two months away.

Today, Leesa wanted to meet with the caterer to confirm the menu. I stepped outside and sat in a rocking chair on the front porch to wait for her arrival. It was the perfect day for being outdoors. The April weather had been breezy all week. Best enjoy it because summer temperatures along with high humidity would barge in before its designated time. Spring seemed to last only a few weeks in the South despite the calendar dates.

My husband, Amos Jones, whipped around the front yard with his favorite toy. I grinned and waved at him. I'd never imagined after my first husband passed that I would marry again. Amos lived next door and a widow himself, he had become the neighborhood yard guy. He'd grabbed my attention back then, reminding me that life wasn't over just because I was a widow, retired and an empty nester. I learned really fast that my hormones were still working just fine.

Amos eased up close to the front porch on his lawnmower and cut the engine. "Where y'all heading today?"

"Smokin' Ward. You know Leesa's friends have been catering for a while, but they acquired a food truck a year ago."

Amos swung his legs around on the lawnmower and stood. "Yeah. And they serve barbecue, right?"

I nodded. Another one of my favorite memories involved my father, a quiet and reserved man, somewhat like Amos. My dad and his brothers would smoke a whole hog out in the backyard, one of the benefits of living out in the country. He cooked some of the best barbecue. To this day, I was still biased about my daddy's cooking.

I explained to Amos. "Smokin' Ward specializes in giving people the barbecue they like best, whether it's vinegar based or tomato based. Leesa said they just won a culinary award. Want me to bring you a plate back?"

Amos wiped his brow with a handkerchief. "Yes, ma'am. I will be ready for some down home cooking after I finish these yards. Make sure they add some hash and rice, too."

Amos claimed he was a city boy, but that man loved to eat good ole country food. I knew he would work up quite an appetite. He still owned the house next door where his daughter lived, and he kept the lawn to both houses nice and neat. He even helped out our next door neighbor, Louise Hopkins.

I turned as Leesa pulled her minivan into our driveway. "Well, there's the bride. I didn't know how super organized that child was until she started handing out tasks to do for this wedding." I stood from the rocking chair and made my way down the steps. "That girl has a checklist for everything."

Amos grabbed my hand and helped me down the last few steps. "Like mother, like daughter. You love your notebooks too," he grinned.

I threw my head back and laughed. "That's true."

I walked over and opened the passenger side door. My daughter leaned forward and waved at Amos who'd followed behind me. "Hey, Amos," Leesa said. "You have these yards looking so good."

"Thank you. I appreciate the compliment." Amos inquired. "So I hear you are having barbecue at your wedding."

Leesa grinned. "My friend Sasha and her husband are excellent cooks. We're going to have a whole soul food menu. Both Chris's family and mine love to eat."

"We absolutely do." I agreed as I climbed into her minivan.

Amos waved and headed back toward his lawnmower.

I waited until Leesa backed out of the driveway. "How long do you have for lunch today? Are we going to be able to get everything accomplished?"

A big grin stretched across Leesa's face. "I have the afternoon off, so no worries."

I raised an eyebrow. "Well, that sounds like a plan."

In just a few minutes, we'd reached the Sugar Creek business district. Across the street were Sugar Creek Cafe and a few shops. Leesa passed them and turned into a parking lot next to a furniture store.

Before I opened the car door, I could smell the savory aroma of smoked barbecue in the air. My stomach rumbled, already tasting the sweet and tangy sauce that would soon coat my fingers. "Mmmm, it smells good out here."

When we rounded the corner of the parking lot, I saw the BBQ Fix truck first. That struck me as odd. "I thought we were going to Sasha's truck."

Leesa frowned. "It's over there. You know what. Sasha told me last night that the guy who owns BBQ Fix has been setting up shop wherever they are lately. It's really weird, because Sasha and her husband Marcus book with businesses and organizations in advance to be able to sell food. No one wants two barbecue food trucks in the same location."

"That is weird. Sounds like someone is trying to strike up a bit of competition."

Leesa mentioned, "Well, he won that culinary award the past two years. Sasha said the man was really upset about losing to them."

Usually when I saw Sasha Greene she wore her thick curly hair in a fierce fro. Today it was tied back with an emerald scarf. Her hair had always been deep auburn, but I could tell she'd added a bit more red to her natural coloring.

Leesa walked up to the window. "Hey, Sasha. What's going on?"

Sasha shook her head. "I don't know. Marcus went to tell Damien to move his truck. This is the second time this week he's pulled this stunt. There is plenty of room for both of our trucks to serve food in Charleston."

I turned around and looked at the other truck. "Are you sure it's a good idea for Marcus to go over there? That guy might be itching to start a fight."

Sasha's face scrunched up as she bit her lip. "I tried to stop him, but you know men." She squinted and said, "Well, it looks like he's coming back."

Marcus Green sprinted back across the parking lot to where we stood by the Smokin' Ward truck. His face appeared strained.

I asked, "Marcus, is everything okay?"

Leesa added, "Yeah, was that guy giving you a hard time?"

Marcus stopped and put his hands on his hips. Then he bent down like he was about to hyperventilate.

"Honey, are you okay?" A concerned Sasha opened the back door of the food truck and climbed out. We all stood around Marcus wondering what was wrong.

Finally, sounding out of breath he said. "I went over to ask Damien to move his truck. He didn't answer, so I walked around and the truck's door was wide open. We may need to call 9-1-1."

"Oh," I said. "Is he hurt?" I reached into my bag and pulled out my phone. "Well, what should we tell them?"

Marcus shook his head. "I don't know. He looks like he's not breathing."

"What?" Leesa and I yelled at the same time.

Before I could stop her, Leesa started walking toward the BBQ Fix truck. "Leesa," I shouted. "Where are you going?" I found myself scurrying behind her.

"To see if the man needs help. I took a CPR class a few months ago."

"Yes, I remember you telling me that."

Leesa said, "Well, if he's not breathing, it could be too late by the time the ambulance gets here."

We reached the truck and hurried around to the back. But before we reached the open doors, I saw two large feet dressed in white sneakers first. Then a full view of the large man's body sprawled on the food truck's floor came into view. I grabbed Leesa and yanked her back. I didn't know what was more convincing, the blood pooling under the man's head or the bluish tinge of his skin. Probably both.

"Leesa, CPR isn't going to help him. We need to call 9-1-1 and stay back."

This was a crime scene.

Click here to read more or go to https://books2read.com/marinatedconditions

About the Author

Tyora Moody is the author of **Soul-Searching Mysteries,** which includes **cozy mystery, women sleuth mystery, and mystery romance** under the Christian Fiction genre. Her books include the Eugeena Patterson Mysteries, Joss Miller Mysteries, Serena Manchester Mysteries, Reed Family Mysteries, and the Victory Gospel Mysteries.

In 2022, she began writing books for children under her pen name, T.M. Moody.

When Tyora isn't working for a literary client, she's either loving on her cats, listening to an audiobook or podcast, binge-watching crime shows or Marvel movies, and of course, thinking about the next book.

To contact Tyora about reviewing her books or book club discussions, visit her online at TyoraMoody.com.

Join her newsletter at https://tyoramoody.substack.com/

Also By Tyora Moody

Eugeena Patterson Mysteries

Deep Fried Trouble, #1

Oven Baked Secrets, #2

Lemon Filled Disaster, #3

A Simmering Dilemma, #4

An Unsavory Mess, #5

A Spicy Predicament, #6

Marinated Conditions, #7

Eugeena Patterson Family Shorts

Shattered Dreams, #1

A Blended Family Christmas, #2

Falling in Love... Again!, #3

Joss Miller Mysteries
Double Mocha Blues, #1
A Latte Mayhem, #2

Serena Manchester Mysteries
Hostile Eyewitness, prequel
Bittersweet Motives, #1
Dangerous Confessions, #2
Waning Innocence, #3
Presumed Guilty, #4

Reed Family Mysteries
Broken Heart, #1
Troubled Heart, #2
Relentless Heart, #3
Faithful Heart, #4
Wounded Heart, #5

Victory Gospel Series (Mysteries)
When Rain Falls, #1
When Memories Fade, #2
When Perfection Fails, #3

Victory Gospel Shorts (Sweet Romance)
The Replacement Date, #1
Southern Delights, #2
When Love Finds Me, #3

A SPICY PREDICAMENT